A RACE AGAINST TIME

VIRTUAL REALITY
BOOK 1

A RACE
AGAINST
TIME

A Novel

William Kritlow

Publishers Since 1798

THOMAS NELSON PUBLISHERS
Nashville • Atlanta • London • Vancouver

Copyright © 1995 by William Kritlow

Published in Nashville, Tennessee, by Thomas Nelson, Inc., Publishers, and distributed in Canada by Word Communications, Ltd., Richmond, British Columbia, and in the United Kingdom by Word (UK), Ltd., Milton Keynes, England.

Scripture quotations are from the NEW KING JAMES VERSION of the Bible. Copyright © 1979, 1980, 1982, Thomas Nelson, Inc., Publishers.

Library of Congress Cataloging-in-Publication Data

Kritlow, William.
    A race against time : a novel / William Kritlow.
        p. cm. — (The virtual reality series ; bk. 1)
    Summary: Kelly and her brother Tim accompany their uncle, an eccentric computer genius, on a dangerous mission using an advanced virtual reality chamber, where they must rely not only on logic, but on their Christian faith, to survive.
    ISBN 0-7852-7923-7 (pbk.)
    [1. Virtual reality—Fiction. 2.Christian life—Fiction. 3. Brothers and sisters—Fiction. 4. Computers—Fiction. 5. Science fiction.]
I. Title. II. Series: Kritlow, William. Virtual reality series ; bk. 1.
PZ7.K914Rac   1995
[Fic]—dc20   94-43192
                                                                      CIP
                                                                      AC

Printed in the United States of America
1 2 3 4 5 6 7 - 01 00 99 98 97 96 95

C H A P T E R 1

Images came alive inside the helmet's black visor as Hammond Helbert latched it down below his chin. Painted and repainted thirty times a second by his brother's powerful computer, brilliant colors ignited, and a landscape of frantic movement sprang up all around him. Hammond suddenly experienced animation so pure, rapid, and all-encompassing that within a blink of his eye everything outside the helmet ceased to exist—and the images that now arrested his senses became his world—his new reality.

But it wasn't what he expected.

His first surprise came when his black, full-body "reality" suit still worked. Ten years ago he'd helped his younger brother, Matthew, develop the beginnings of this *true* "Virtual Reality," but after their feud erupted he took it for granted that Matthew had canceled his access. But obviously he hadn't because the suit still "spoke" to the computer a few miles away.

Hammond also had assumed that Matthew would program a "virtual world" more in keeping with both their personalities—dreary castles surrounded by moats alive with slithering crocodiles; catacombs of musky, dimly lit passageways, stone walls dripping with molds; and everything controlled by dark sorcerers eager to ensnare the uninvited visitor. That would have been fun, even challenging.

This wasn't. No sorcerers here—only "cute."

Hammond Helbert hated "cute"—this particular "cute" most of all. As he stood at the center of an imaginary town square, live chess pieces scampering frantically around him—he faced an emotional dilemma: He hated "cute" but loved chess.

But there was more to hate. Across the quaint cobblestone street that surrounded the square were nauseatingly quaint little shops—a baker, a cobbler, a small church, and others. All leaned this way and that as if frozen in the middle of a cartoon dance—each stunningly painted in reds, greens, browns, and yellows and each encircled by a garden jammed with blooming blue, yellow, and red flowers. Hammond hated the flowers *and* the houses.

He wished he could conjure up a quaint little bulldozer and flatten it all. But he knew of none. That meant his younger, smarter brother could continue to torment him and Hammond could do nothing to stop him. Hammond would have to grin and bear it.

He sighed. *Matthew, it's good that you're going to die in a few days, or I'd kill you myself.*

He looked around. There were plenty of places to go. Each quaint building had a door he could open, each of the four roads that radiated from the town square led somewhere, and each of the chess pieces had a mouth that could tell him something. But if there were an obvious next step, it didn't immediately present itself.

Worse yet, the obnoxiously happy inhabitants of this obnoxiously happy town were beginning to drive him nuts. They did nothing but run furiously here and there smiling cheerfully. Pawns, rooks, a bishop now and then, knights in full armor galloping nobly upon their midget steeds, all smiled at him as they passed.

Another second and I'll puke, he thought.

A pawn skipped by, a happy grin on the little ball at the tip of his stout little body. Hammond grabbed its neck and lifted its anxious face to his. "Where is it?" he yelled.

The smile turned frightened, then puzzled. The face asked, "What, sire?"

"The formula. Where is it?"

"Formula, sire?"

"Awk!" Hammond spat and threw the pawn to the cobbles. It bounced once, landed on its feet, then, after grinning up at him, scampered off.

A bishop scurried by, his small arms hiking up his base so that his skinny little legs could run freely. He got the same treatment. Violently Hammond's thick hand grabbed the chess piece by the neck and brought the bishop's face to his. "I'm Matthew Helbert's brother, and I've come for the formula. Where is it?"

"Where's Matthew?" the bishop asked.

"He's sick," Hammond growled.

"Sick?" the bishop repeated.

"Where is the formula? Matthew didn't hide it in here and not prepare you to defend it. Now where is it?"

The bishop's eyes narrowed indignantly. "Since we don't really exist—you pose no danger." Then his expression became coolly threatening. "But we may be dangerous to you."

Hammond's brows furled—the bishop was right.

But showing fear wouldn't help—he hardened. "I've no time for your threats. I want the formula now." He suddenly snapped his wrist and the bishop's body dropped to the ground, while his head remained in Hammond's grasp. Robbed of voice, the body ran in circles, its skinny hands searching in vain above its neck.

Still in the cup of Hammond's hand, the head's expression remained cool. "We're not afraid of you here," it said.

"Bah!" Hammond growled and tossed the head to the ground. It bounced once and landed squarely upon the scampering shoulders. Finding its head, the hands clapped joyously as the now-complete bishop darted off.

About to grab another passerby, Hammond suddenly heard a horse snorting like a locomotive behind him and felt bursts of hot breath on his back. He turned. Inches from his face, its nostrils flaring powerfully, stood a massive black horse, its muscles twitching anxiously. As Hammond stared up at its coal black eyes and heard its hooves paw at the cobbles, he told himself that there was nothing to be afraid of—it was all make-believe.

The image of this immense creature was the product of a

clever computer program. The hot breath came from "sensation simulators" triggered by the computer inside the suit and helmet—simulators that Hammond had developed himself. The sound of the horse pawing at the stones was only computer-generated sound. Yet the sight of the huge animal only a heartbeat from pounding him into the earth was powerful and, instinctively, Hammond felt fear.

Atop the horse, clad in glistening silver armor, sat a knight. He peered down at Hammond through small slits in an iron, red-plumed helmet. "You've come to do battle?" the knight asked. "Not sure I like you rippin' the heads off my friends."

"He never used it anyway. I've come for the formula."

"You say our beloved Matthew is sick?"

"In a coma—he's unconscious on the floor of his lab—I was actually talking to him on the teleconferencing hookup when he toppled over."

"And he told you to come here?"

"In a way. He said he'd hidden the formula where I'd never find it. But as he told me this, he kept glancing at the virtual reality computer in the next room. I knew what he meant. I need that formula quickly."

"What made him unconscious—in a coma?"

"The formula. It's a bacterium, or maybe a virus that he developed in his laboratory. He was careless and infected himself. He says it's highly contagious . . . "

"Contagious?"

"Catchy—it passes quickly from person to person, maybe even between animals. Which means he's probably infected others—they'll be falling into comas soon. Then, after three or four days, according to his research, they'll die. Just like he will.

"He's hidden the formula for the process that produces the bacterium and, just as important, the cure for it somewhere in this virtual reality created by his computer. Which I helped him develop," Hammond said, turning completely around and drinking it all in.

"I wanted to create a far-out Disney World and make tons of money. But he wanted to play by himself. Now I'll have the last laugh. I don't need his virtual reality to get rich—I'll blackmail the world by threatening to let the bacterium go—then by selling the cure. Of course, money means nothing to you . . . "

"Nothing," the knight reaffirmed.

"So no need to bribe you. But there's something else. He's probably programmed you to want to survive so this will be important. In three days, when he dies—you die."

The knight straightened. "How?"

"He never trusted me. So he created a brain wave monitor. When his brain waves stop—when he's dead—the computer lets loose a software virus that destroys all this—and you with it."

"Really?"

"Really. Now, where's the formula? Keeping Matthew alive is the only chance you have."

Although Hammond couldn't see the knight's expression behind the iron visor, he knew there was some heavy thinking going on—if that's what a computer making a decision can be called. Suddenly the knight leaned down and motioned Hammond closer. "The formula isn't hidden here," the knight whispered through the metal grate.

"Where then?"

"Understand I'm doing this for all of us here in VR."

"I'm sure Matthew will understand."

The knight's armor squeaked a bit as he nodded. "It's beyond the great wall," he said, his armored hand pointing over Hammond's shoulder. Turning, Hammond saw a cobblestone road that ran between two silly-looking buildings and continued out beyond the town to disappear between the folds in a rolling green countryside.

Hammond began walking. Although he kept himself in good shape, he wasn't built for walking—his legs were short and his feet were small. So, as the miles went by, his feet burned and sweat ran down his cheeks. The wall was a welcome sight when he finally saw it.

The great wall was just that. When still miles away he saw it stretch from horizon to horizon and as high as the skies. It seemed to have no purpose other than to block his way.

But when he got within a few feet of the wall, he saw a small, head-high door in it, and, to his surprise, the door opened at a touch. *Why would Matthew program a wall like that and put an unlocked door in it?* Hammond wondered. *For effect?*

He quickly found out. When the door closed behind him, it locked. He knew because he checked. The moment he saw what waited for him beyond the wall he turned and grabbed the ancient brass knob, but it didn't even jiggle.

Again he recited to himself that everything was just images and sensations, that none of this was real. His recitation didn't help—he was suddenly afraid again.

About ten feet above his head, growing from acres of thickly twisted vines, were the longest, nastiest looking thorns he'd ever seen. The angry needles, their points saber sharp, grew chaotically to form a daggered canopy that stretched to all horizons. In a growing breeze, the thorns clattered menacingly. But they were ten feet over his head, far enough away to only look threatening. Although the world beneath was haunted by dismal, gray shadows, there was nothing really dangerous. *Anyway,* he reminded himself, *the thorns are only imaginary.* His search could continue unhindered.

Actually, he hadn't been standing directly under the thorns. A ribbon of open sky unrolled between the great wall and the jagged canopy, and he stood beneath that. He continued to hesitate, sensing that Matthew reveled in surprises—and a truly nasty surprise could be waiting for him under those thorns. But he could wait no longer. After a few quick breaths, he stepped into the shadows.

Suddenly he experienced a strange and overwhelming sensation—weightlessness. He'd never experienced real weightlessness before, so he wasn't sure if the computer and sensation simulators were representing the feeling accurately, but it didn't matter. He was beginning to rise—he felt it. He saw the ground drop away and the thorns pressing down—both happened quickly.

Totally unprepared, he flailed at the air in a vain attempt to stop his ascent—he even remembered there was an arsenal of guns and knives located somewhere in the program that he could check out like library books and use. But imaginary guns firing imaginary bullets into imaginary thorns would do him no good—all the bullets in the world would do him no good now. The needle-sharp points were closing in. Hammond figured he had two alternatives—he could cover his face to protect it or grab the nearest thorn and propel himself away.

He chose to grab the nearest thorn. His hand closed around it near the point, and he felt its sleek chill. His ascent stopped. But only for a heartbeat—his lower body continued to rise and in another moment a thorn stabbed his leg.

Twisting, he saw a spiked point touch, then tear through his pant leg; red blood oozed from the wound. The thorn, his pants, the wound were all just images projected on the inside of his helmet—but the pain was real. The moment the thorn pierced his leg he felt an excruciating electric shock—so painful that he screamed. He felt a second shock when his other leg strayed and glanced off another thorn. He pulled that leg away, and immediately rammed it into a third barb.

This couldn't go on. Knowing his brother's mind, Hammond knew there was a solution to all this somewhere. But, for the moment, at least, he was too exhausted to look for it. Feeling a bit like a wounded spacecraft, he grabbed a thorn near his head and carefully guided his legs so that they lodged safely between two thorns. He docked himself there, resting.

As he monitored the safety of his body parts, Hammond did what he always did when confronted with a difficult problem—he thought about it. In a few minutes, he had formulated a plan.

When the infection Matthew carries begins to strike others, he thought, *health officials will track the origin of the disease to Matthew's lab and find him unconscious on the floor. Then the people Matthew has been working with—all those highly placed, powerful government people—will come to the same conclusion I have. They will search Matthew's little invention—virtual reality—for the formula. Since they've been working with him closely, they will probably know where the formula is—or at least how to find it.*

Hammond's plan was simple—find a way out of these thorns, do a little investigating on his own, then return and wait for those coming next to lead him to what he sought. Then he'd take it—violently if necessary. After all, he knew about them, but they knew nothing about him.

Tim Craft, a tall, lanky fourteen year old, his blond hair
mussed by a growing breeze, was searching for Kelly, his
thirteen-year-old sister. They were staying on their Uncle
Morty's farm while their parents were away, and after he
scoured his uncle's two-story house, he stretched his long
legs toward the duck pond out back. Not finding her on
the swing beneath the sprawling elm, he climbed the distant knoll and scanned his parents' alfalfa fields, his own
house a distant spike on the horizon.

Just as he was about to turn back to the farm buildings,
he heard the crunch of tires on the long, dirt drive. He saw
a black Ford Taurus come to a stop in front of Morty's house
and a tall, slender man with black hair and dark blue suit
and tie get out. Before stepping onto Morty's porch the man
stood for a moment looking around.

"Can I help you?" Tim called to the visitor.

The visitor was obviously not used to the humidity of a
Wisconsin summer. He dabbed his brow with a handkerchief
before replying. "Is Morty Craft here?"

"I think he's painting the barn," Tim replied, walking
toward the car.

"That must be something to see."

"It's the barn that's something to see."

"I'm Mike Dunhill—FBI."

"Tim Craft—Morty's my uncle."

"Nice to meet you." Mike extended a hand, and Tim
shook it. "I need to talk to him."

"FBI?" Tim had never spoken to an FBI agent before and suddenly felt a little nervous. "I guess I need to find him. It could take a while."

"I've got time—it's important."

A thought came to Tim, "Hey, what did Uncle Morty used to do for you guys? It's a big mystery around here."

"He worked with computers—that's all I can say."

Tim nodded and glanced toward the house. Uncle Morty's very powerful computer hummed in the back room—a gift from an unnamed branch of the U.S. Government.

"Oh," Tim said, "I'll go find him."

"I'll come with you."

◱

Morty Craft was feeling foolish. Wheat brown hair with chiseled features, he shared his tall, thin build with Tim. Right now a bucket of yellow paint was lodged upside down on Morty's head. Yellow sheets oozed down his neck, shoulders, arms, and inside his overalls. He hadn't even seen it coming.

Although Morty's neighbors tended toward red for their barns, about a week ago an artistic thought had struck him. He'd paint his barn blue, with billowing clusters of white clouds. For dramatic effect, he'd paint some with black underbellies spitting brilliant yellow lightning. He'd already finished the blue and the white clouds. Now it was time for dark underbellies and lightning. Earlier in the day he had interrupted his painting to try welding together old tractor parts with chicken wire to create something quite innovative. He'd started that project in the toolshed in back of the barn, but in the middle of that an inspiration for two clouds having a lightning duel broke over him.

He had mixed the yellow paint with just a hint of red to give it a fiery look, leaned his tallest ladder against the barn wall, and climbed. He was near the top when he realized he'd forgotten the paintbrush. He set the bucket on a narrow window ledge and headed back down. On his way down, two of his eight dogs, the black chow and the beagle, got into a frenzied squabble near the base of the ladder and chased each other into the barn wall. They immediately disappeared, but the shock dislodged the paint can and . . .

The paint was bad enough, but trying to find his way down the twenty-foot ladder while removing the can presented another challenge.

"Uncle Morty?" Tim called. And Mike rounded the side of the barn just in time to see the paint can hit its mark and now stood at the base of the ladder trying to both hold the ladder steady and avoid the still dripping yellow. "What happened?"

"Tim? Oh, praise God. Grab the ladder while I get this can off my head."

"I got it," Tim told him, and Morty worked on the can. "I don't think Picasso ever had problems like this, Uncle Morty?!"

"Picasso never painted barns." Morty tried to laugh, but it came out a groan.

Although he wasn't as tall or as muscular as his brother, Morty still cut an energetic figure. That energy now struggled to break the paint can free. When he finally succeeded, the paint sealed above his head broke loose, and a fresh curtain of it washed over him. Now he looked a bit dampened. His brown hair was streaked with running yellow, and his deep brown eyes peered from beneath dripping brows. "Towels," he said, "I need towels."

At that moment the stream of paint before his eyes parted, and he saw Mike Dunhill. Morty's mouth dropped, but before he could say anything a river of dogs flowed, barking and howling, around the far end of the barn. There were three beagles, a black chow that looked more like a lion, and four terriers of various kinds. They were all on the heels of Shivers, a big, caramel-colored cat.

"I don't know why they do it. They never have a chance," Morty said, eyes still on his old friend. "Mike," he greeted excitedly, "a blast from the past." He pushed paint away from his eyes. "Mike was my 'big brother' in college," he told Tim.

"Looks to me like you still need one." Mike smiled, shaking his head.

"What's a 'big brother' do?" Tim asked.

"I was only ten when I started MIT, got my Ph.D. at fourteen. I needed a much, much older guy to keep me from hurting myself. I missed a lot of growing up—maybe that's why I paint barns the way I do now."

"I'm only a few years older," Mike explained. "But I'm much wiser. I went to the FBI, and he went into computers until I finally convinced him to use that brain for the government."

"You're not here just for fun, Mike. What's on your mind?"

"First get cleaned up. I talk to no man dripping with paint. Then I need to bend your ear in private."

"Fortunately this stuff is water-based. We can talk in my study."

Tim chuckled as the clownish yellow figure and his "big brother" headed for the house.

"What happened to him?" a voice came from behind him. "And who's the man in the suit?

Tim turned to see Kelly standing at the sliding barn door. Her sky blue eyes reflected highlights from her flowered blouse and jeans, while auburn hair cascaded down her shoulders, fluttering slightly in the breeze. In her hand was a letter.

"He's Morty's FBI friend," Tim answered.

"FBI? What's he want?"

Tim shrugged. "Who knows."

"I guess we'll find out if we're supposed to," Kelly said turning toward the barn. Tim followed, and she took a seat on a bale of hay just where a long dusty shaft of light from a high window hit.

Tim plopped down on the hay bale beside her. "Who's the letter from?"

"Mom and Dad," Kelly answered.

"Really? Where are they now?"

"England," she said as she dropped the pages dreamily into her lap. "I can't believe they didn't take me."

"It's their second honeymoon. No way they'd take either of us."

"But they left so suddenly—"

"Uncle Morty's been here several months now—I guess they figured he could look after us."

"I think it's more like us looking after him," Kelly said.

"For someone so smart . . . "

Kelly suddenly interrupted, "There's a rumor going around."

"What rumor?"

"You know very well what rumor," Kelly said, eying him suspiciously.

Tim suddenly became sullen. "Rumor's right. It happened." He sighed, glancing at a book that lay beside Kelly.

"So the grapevine tells the truth. She dumped you."

"Sondra Walker," he let the name fall off his tongue. "She was something."

"Sondra," Kelly emphasized the "o" sound with great drama, "could seed clouds with that nose of hers—she keeps it so high in the air. You should say good riddance. How'd she do it?"

"I showed up at her place this morning, and this guy was there . . ."

"Classy," Kelly said. "How do you feel?"

"Pretty stupid," Tim admitted as he took her book and thumbed idly through it. "She *was* beautiful."

"She was *not* a Christian—nowhere near," Kelly said as she put her face very close to Tim's. "She lures foolish boys to their doom. You should be glad."

"Well, she won't lure this guy anymore."

Kelly patted his leg. "Cassy Briggs told me last night that she sorta likes you."

"Cassy?" He said the name with little enthusiasm. "She's okay, I guess."

"She's nice."

"I guess." He wasn't biting. He thumbed the pages of her book and asked, "What place are you mooning over this time?"

Kelly allowed a certain longing to wash over her. "Do you think there really are other places besides Chippewa Falls, Wisconsin?"

"You mean out in the real world?"

"Out there, yes," she said, her hand sweeping past the open barn door. "I bet people sit on real chairs on real patios with gardens—and the smell of hay and cows is always somewhere else. Do you think places like that really exist?"

"Where's this book take you?"

"Prince Edward Island," she said, eyes coming back to him.

"You'd be too afraid to go!" Tim laughed.

"What's that supposed to mean?" Kelly fired back.

"It means you're afraid to fly. You're afraid to get on a boat. We live near a lake, and you've been on it twice, I think. Long walks probably give you hives."

"I take lots of long walks," Kelly argued. "Trains—I could take trains."

"To Prince Edward Island?" Tim groaned. "You'd have to find one with water wings."

"I'd just have to face my fears," she said with great resolve. But the thought of facing them frightened her. She'd been on one plane flight in her life when she went on a school trip to Florida. The moment the plane door closed, her heart began to pound and the blood settled in her shoes. Even on a trip to the Wisconsin Dells the moment she stepped on the boat, she memorized where the life vests were. Her fears were real.

"Funny, isn't it?" Tim mused.

"What is?"

"We live in Chippewa Falls, Wisconsin, home of Cray Research, builder of the fastest computers in the world with some of the most exotic technologies, and you have to read books and I have to do puzzles for entertainment. Where is my puzzle book anyway?" he asked. He liked the logic puzzles best. "Of course," he continued, "there's always Uncle Morty."

A year ago their father's brother had fled his life in Washington, D.C.—a life he couldn't talk about—and bought the farm next to theirs. Since then, Uncle Morty had gained the reputation among the local farmers as just a bit eccentric. Even those who worked for Cray found him a little off center.

"Do you think we ought to tell Mom and Dad about the fire?"

Two days before they'd almost been burned alive when a welding torch set one of the outbuildings on fire. They knew that their mom probably would have forgiven Uncle Morty had he been diligently welding a piece of farm machinery, but he hadn't. He was creating something artistic from pieces of an old tractor—something even Tim and Kelly found a little grotesque—something their mom wouldn't understand—something no one in Chippewa Falls would understand.

"She'd turn the blowtorch on him."

"I miss them," Kelly said, eyes suddenly downcast.

"I suppose I do too. But being here has given me a lot of time with Uncle Morty's computer."

"That's an understatement. You're always playing with it."

Tim loved Morty's computer. Uncle Morty, on the other hand, both loved and hated it. He fled to the country specifically to escape "the silicon monsters," as he called them. But late at night, after a day that didn't quite go the way he wanted, Morty would slip into the computer room off his living room and work—sometimes until dawn. Tim had recently spent one of those nights with him, and he'd loved it.

"Uncle Morty's been talking to that guy a long time," Kelly said.

"He's an old friend—Mike-something. FBI. I said that, didn't I?"

At that moment they heard the distant squeal of the screen door on the porch. Then it slapped.

Kelly grinned. "Time's come to find out what's going on."

A moment later, yellow paint still smeared on his face and neck where he'd tried to wipe it off, Morty poked his head into the barn. Mike followed him in.

"Great, now we find out. What does the FBI want with you, Uncle Morty?" Although Kelly asked the question with a mischievous smile on her face she received a serious look from Morty in reply. "Mike won't tell me the specifics yet, but they need my peculiar talents," he said.

"For what?" Tim asked.

"I can't tell you right now," Mike said. "And I'm not going to say anything else until Morty gets a bath. The FBI has its standards." He laughed, but then he, too, became serious. "We've got a plane waiting for us at Eau Claire airport." Mike took a deep breath as if preparing to say something difficult. "Your uncle says he's responsible for you guys. I don't like it, but he's convinced me that you need to come along."

"If I'm going—you're going," said Uncle Morty. "I can't leave you here alone."

"Really?" Now Kelly stood.

"Don't make too much of this," Mike injected. "You'll probably be bored silly."

"But there's no one else to leave you with, and I'm responsible—so you're coming." There were times on the farm when Morty looked lost—completely out of place. This was not one of those times. He was completely in charge. "Tim, call that handy-guy who's taking care of your folks' place, and ask him to feed my dogs and the herd . . . "

"Herd?" Tim smiled. "You have one cow."

"Herds vary in size," Uncle Morty pointed out. "Now, get packed—pack light."

"Figure you'll be gone about a week," Mike told them. "And —it's a small plane."

The kids caught their breath as if afraid they might cheer by accident. "A week? No problem!" Tim said, all but leaping toward the barn door.

"Small plane?" Kelly went green.

A short time later, while his Uncle Morty scrubbed himself in the shower, Tim set his heavy suitcase at the top of the stairs and stepped into Kelly's room.

"I can't believe it. Espionage," he said, rubbing his hands together excitedly.

"What?"

"FBI, CIA . . . spies . . . all that stuff."

"You're nuts. He'll probably be stuck in a basement somewhere with a bunch of computers, and we *will* be bored to tears." She grabbed a small carry-on bag she had brought with her. "I'm stuffing this bag with books—very exotic books that are about very exotic places. And you'd better grab some puzzle books. I think you're going to need them." She plopped down on her bed. "I know I will—to take my mind off that small plane. They crash all the time."

"Do you realize we're related to that genius down there— Ph.D. from MIT at fourteen? His blood is coursing through our veins. Didn't Dad tell us to use our talents for the Lord?"

"Yeah, I guess. If we survive the plane ride."

Each Craft handed Mike a suitcase and he, in turn, stuffed them into the trunk of the black Taurus. Then each took a last look at the farm—the kids as if they hoped they might never come back, Uncle Morty as if he was leaving a place of safety. Then they all got into the car and drove to the Eau Claire airport.

A Lear jet was waiting for them at a small terminal at the airport's perimeter. As they approached, as if by magic, steps unfolded, and the four of them climbed aboard. The interior was awash with patriotism, red flooring, blue walls, and white seats. The FBI emblem—a shield surrounded by thirteen stars, surrounded by a sunburst—blazed golden on the partition separating them from the flight crew. Seating was simple: a lounge area surrounding a small, low table and a few rows of standard airplane seats in the back. Although the plane was small the cabin afforded adequate head room. When they were seated around the table, Mike said, "We'll talk when we get airborne. Strap yourselves in."

Seconds later they had complied, especially Kelly, who pulled the belt extra tight—then tighter still when the door closed. Wrapping white knuckles around the ends of the armrests, she felt as prepared as she'd ever be. Tim gently patted her on the leg, but she didn't feel it. Then Mike hit a button on his armrest. "Ready," he said.

A voice replied over a microphone, "On our way."

The engines whined, and Kelly gasped and grabbed Tim's

hand. Seeing her panic, Morty took her other hand and whispered, "Prayer helps. We're in God's hands."

Moments later they were airborne, and a few minutes after that they bumped through some clouds, then leveled off above them.

The engines whined and at forty thousand feet the Lear jet laced through rare atmosphere, the world a blur beneath. Mike stood and faced the little group. "Let me act the host, first. Can I get drinks for everyone?"

"Coke, please," Tim said, and Kelly, still petrified, nodded. Morty asked for a club soda, and Mike got himself coffee.

Tim unzipped the carry-on bag and rummaged inside. A moment later he had a crossword puzzle by his side while Kelly found a book she hoped would take her someplace far away from airplanes.

CHAPTER 3

M orty turned to Mike. "Now, what's this really all about?"

Mike lowered his voice and sat next to Morty. The moment he did, the kids' books dropped and their ears perked. "We've got a problem—the world has a problem."

"And?" Morty sounded assured, direct.

"Remember Matthew Helbert?"

"This has to do with him?" Morty noticed an inquisitive look spread across Tim's face. "Dr. Matthew Helbert and I were rivals at MIT. We were about the same age and had the same interests. The competition between us got brutal. When brains is all you have and someone has more brains than you do, you can think of yourself as a lesser human being. Brutal."

As the kids nodded their understanding, Morty went on, "Because of Matthew I pursued my Ph.D. all the more vigorously."

"You beat him by a year," Mike pointed out.

"While he lumbered along as an old man of fifteen I got the fellowship at Stanford then went to the National Security Agency."

"At fifteen he went to Livermore, Sandia, and Los Alamos," Mike continued.

"Matthew had broader interests than I did. Where I stuck with international stuff, he not only designed computers, but he worked in biochemistry, molecular modeling, and weapons research. His overriding love was always computer simulation though. That's where he and I had a lot in common."

"Simulation?" Kelly asked.

"That's when you make the computer calculate how the real world would act. For instance, if you wanted the computer to simulate a ball bouncing, you'd program it to understand the ball's elastic properties and tell it how hard it will hit the ground. From all that you can tell how high it will bounce—you simulate what you know and gain new information as well. It can get complex very quickly.

"This plane we're in, for example, was probably designed using a computer to calculate, or simulate, air flow over and under its wings to understand its properties of lift, and around its fuselage to understand drag, and over the whole thing to understand stability. That way they could determine the most efficient design without putting an actual model through a lot of expensive wind tunnel tests.

"Also, the computer is more accurate because rather than showing air flow etched in colored oils over the fuselage, it produces numerical results. The data is displayed on a graphics workstation. That particular application is called computational fluid dynamics."

Morty formed a frustrated smile. "I just heard myself. I branched into my professional voice, didn't I? Sometimes I think I'm two people."

"Well, it's the one who understands all that and knows Helbert who we want right now," Mike said. "That's why you're here."

"Where are we going?" Kelly asked.

"San Diego," Mike said. "Recently Helbert built a private lab as part of the University of San Diego—right between the San Diego Supercomputer Center and Scripps Research."

"They both have Crays," Morty said.

Mike's brows furled. "Crays?"

"Cray Research Supercomputers. They're manufactured in Chippewa, where you found us. They run at billions of instructions per second. I consulted for them for a while. Good people. Scripps does biochem and molecular modeling—that's another term for simulation—and the supercomputer center does it all. That's a lot of power for Helbert to be playing with. He was brilliant, but something always seemed dangerous about him—that competitive streak was very fierce."

"You too," Mike said.

"Once. Not so much anymore."

"But even though Helbert was part of our threesome," Mike began, "we really didn't get close until I busted his brother several years ago."

"Hammond?" Morty asked. "He was sixteen when I graduated."

"He turned out about as smart as Matthew, only he went into crime. He became a high-tech thief."

"Really?" Morty said with thoughtful surprise.

"Hammond Helbert?" Kelly let the unusual name roll off her tongue. She was beginning to relax a little. "With a name like that no wonder he turned out bad."

Morty smiled and said, "The competition Matthew and I had was child's play compared to what he had with his brother. They hated each other. Fought constantly, and tried to outdo each other at every opportunity. Had something to do with their father financing Matthew's education and then having nothing left for Hammond—there were probably other problems too. But whatever the reason, when they got together sparks flew. Trouble was, they seemed to get together a lot. In fact, I think they even tried to work together at one point, but of course that didn't last long."

Tim asked Mike, "What did you catch Hammond for?"

"Hammond tapped into a bank's computer, and as the interest on people's accounts was being calculated he had all the round-off amounts deposited into his account. It accumulated fast. After about a year's effort I snared him. Matthew loved the fact that I'd nailed his brother, and from then on he and I were tight. He'd write me at least once every couple weeks." Mike's brows furled and he added, "Just like he did two days ago."

Kelly glanced for the umpteenth time out the window. This time she saw another jet not far off their wing. It wasn't close enough for her to see the pilot, but it was close enough for her to say, "Aren't planes supposed to keep some distance between them?"

The moment she said it, the plane slid closer.

Mike saw it and quickly hit the intercom. "What's going on off the starboard?"

Before the pilot answered, the jet closed in and peeled off then disappeared behind them as if diving for their tail. The intercom crackled, "The guy's nuts."

Suddenly the plane was back, this time across and in back of Kelly. Fear returned to Kelly and came to all of them.

Mike hit the button again. "Any idea who?"

"No, but it's something you don't see every day—a single pilot Paris II-B jet. It can seat four. No numbers," came the reply. "Captain's calling Omaha to get some help. They usually can't move like that. Must be modified."

The jet fell back slightly and shadowed them.

Eyes tense, Mike said, "We'll have a couple of fighters up here in a second or two. In the meantime, I'll continue. Two days ago a strange disease broke out."

"I can feel where this is going," Morty said.

Mike reached into his suit coat pocket and pulled out a small notebook. "People around Morro Bay, California, started slipping into comas. The first one was Maddie Walsh, thirty-five years old with a fourteen-year-old daughter—"

"The daughter too?" Morty asked.

"No. She seems to be okay. There were a couple of others around there. When those three fell unconscious within just a few minutes of one another, it was reported to Disease Control in Sacramento. Not long thereafter five people near a small lake in the hills—one of them, a fifty-eight year old named Will Stark, who was driving a truck at the time—also fell into comas."

He slipped the notebook back into his pocket and went on, "I got a letter from Helbert the day these people were dropping, telling me he just got back from a trip to Morro Bay where he'd done some fishing."

"And he'd just done something incredible with recombinant DNA and produced a new something or other . . ." Morty glanced out one of the portholes at the jet beside them.

"He's written papers describing his work in that area. Some of it is quite unique." Morty's expression darkened as he continued, "Matthew messing around with that stuff is frightening. It takes a thorough understanding, a meticulous commitment to detail and safety. Matthew never did things that way—he had a gunslinger's attitude." Morty leaned back and rubbed his eyes, a flake of paint coming off on his fingers. How distant the morning seemed now. "But there's another reason to be concerned," he said.

"That is?"

"Matthew always seemed angry, like life had cheated him. He always seemed to want to get back at people. He'd mistreat lab animals—perform tests on them that would hurt them needlessly. He'd abuse fellow students and lab workers. Even the professors weren't immune. Matthew was brilliant, but I always thought he'd destroy the world if he had half the chance. He'd do better on a short leash rather than with two supercomputers to play with."

"My boss asked if I thought he'd do this on purpose. I said no. Do you disagree?"

"I might," Morty said grimly.

"What's recombinant DNA?" Tim asked.

"DNA is the code the Lord put into every animal cell. It describes the organism's physical characteristics. Alter, or 'recombine' the code, and most of the time you just kill the organism. Sometimes, however, you hit a combination that will produce a new organism. The problem comes when that new organism produces a detrimental—uh—bad effect and there's no immunity. That's what seems to have happened here. People are infected, and they can't fight it off. And it sounds extremely contagious."

"Eight new cases this morning," Mike said. "We're doing our best to keep a lid on this thing until we know more—until we find the cure."

Morty asked, "How long has Matthew been in the coma?"

"We found him that way on the floor of his lab. And how did you know?" Mike asked but then answered his own question. "Of course you'd know. Why else would we be talking to you?"

Suddenly the jet behind them slid closer. It loomed large and dangerous off the port wing. Mike hit the button. "What's going on with him?"

"Don't know. Omaha's going to take some time. We'll just have to live with him for a while."

"No way to tell who he is?"

"There are no numbers, and he doesn't answer my calls."

Without replying, Mike let the button go and sent a worried look toward the plane.

"The Lord's in control," Morty said. Mike looked back at Morty and said, "I forgot, you're religious."

"The Lord's important to me," Morty said simply.

"Right," Tim reaffirmed.

Mike said nothing but again glared at the plane. Its wing was dangerously close to their own. As if reading Mike's mind, the pilot eased the plane away, lengthening the distance between them.

"Are the folks from Scripps Research involved?"

"They've been running all sorts of tests on Helbert. He's in the clinic's communicable disease ward under tight security. I told them to put him in a steel drum and nail the lid shut, but they wouldn't. So far nothing."

Kelly threw another anxious glance at the jet.

Mike went on, "We need you to perform some of your computer magic."

"How so?"

"Matthew's letter to me also said that he'd created a cure—an antibiotic or something."

"If it's a virus, finding a cure is no mean trick. That's why we still have the common cold."

"He's hidden all the information about the organism or virus, or whatever, somewhere. Because he's a computer jockey like you, we think he's got it somewhere in his bank of computers. We've checked his computer files at Scripps Research and at the supercomputer center, but nothing. It has to be in the lab somewhere. We want you to find it."

"Uncle Morty, do you mind if I ask a question?" Tim injected. When Morty shook his head, Tim asked, "Why did he hide it?"

Mike responded with the sting of irritation, "Because it's obviously dangerous, and he doesn't want the wrong people to find it."

"Tim's question is a good one," Morty said. "It's conceivable that he didn't know how dangerous or contagious it was. Who would be after it?"

Mike only shrugged, his attention again pulled away by their reckless companion. As if suddenly responding to their gaze, the jet peeled away. The reason came rising from below; two F-16s barreled by and, amid trailing thunder, pursued the jet into the clouds. "I guess that takes care of him." Mike chuckled triumphantly.

"Maybe," Morty said, his expression still dark.

Tim felt an electric chill course through him. He'd never seen such a look from Morty.

Kelly saw it too. The infection was spreading. The cure was hidden somewhere by a genius. Maybe the world really was depending on them. *Lord, you are in control, aren't you?* she wondered.

Suddenly Morty's hand slapped his forehead. He'd remembered something. "You got a telephone in this thing?"

"Sure, why?"

"Where is it?"

Mike pushed another button, and a phone appeared from beneath a small end table next to him. "Use it like a car phone."

Morty grabbed it, pressed in the numbers, and hit "send." Self-conscious that he tended to need the fire department more often than the average farmer, Morty addressed the fire chief with the deepest respect a moment later when he spoke. "Mr. Williams? Will you head over to my barn with your fire engine? I left my torch going in my toolshed—in back of the barn—and by now . . ."

"Mr. Williams is the chief of our volunteer fire department," Tim explained to Mike.

"Uncle Morty knows the number by heart," Kelly added. Mike nodded understandingly.

"Yes, the blue barn—no, they're clouds."

He waited impatiently.

"Yes, most barns *are* red."

Another few words from Chippewa.

"No, you may not let it burn—now, on your way, Mr. Williams." Uncle Morty pressed "end" and eyed the others. "Everyone's a critic." He sighed.

The kids suppressed smiles. Uncle Morty was still Uncle Morty no matter if the world *was* coming to an end.

As if to bring them back to their mission, the pilot's voice came over the intercom. "Omaha reports they lost him. He must have been burning some kind of soup in those engines. He disappeared in the mountains."

"You said this wasn't dangerous," Morty confronted Mike gravely.

"Maybe I lied," Mike replied uncomfortably.

"Maybe you shouldn't do that," Morty told Mike.

"You had to come."

Morty was silent.

With the thought that their friend in the jet might be back, if not in the air perhaps on the ground, the kids brought out their books. Tim managed to pursue a logic problem half-heartedly, but Kelly's eyes never made it past the first page.

CHAPTER 4

Reaching San Diego took three hours and change. A local agent met them at Lindbergh Field near downtown San Diego. He introduced himself as Agent Tom Howard and after an efficient handshake led them to the minivan parked outside the terminal.

They headed north on Highway 5 for about eight miles then turned west on Genesee. After climbing a steep hill they came to Torrey Pines Road and University of California, San Diego. A sprawling academic city of irregularly shaped buildings, the college was packed tightly on a broad slope that dropped quickly to the city of La Jolla and the Pacific Ocean. To the left of the intersection was the four-story San Diego Supercomputer Center, and to the right was the two-story Scripps Research Clinic. On the opposite side of Torrey Pines, in a grove of eucalyptus trees, stood Dr. Helbert's lab. High-speed microwave dishes stood atop all three buildings.

They turned into the lab's parking area.

"Who financed all this?" Morty asked as they pulled to a stop beside a white Toyota. Two Marines in snappy green with white gloves blocked their path until Mike produced identification. Then they were permitted to continue.

"It's only a pillbox," Morty exclaimed, "but I guess Helbert never did need much room."

"Although Matthew is wealthy, most of this came from a private source. ChemTech."

Morty nodded. They were a small biochemical house in northern California. "What do you know out about them?"

"Nothing yet. We should get some data soon."

"Those marines aren't going to stop the disease," Morty said as they stepped from the rental van.

"The lab is divided into two areas. The wet lab, where Helbert was found, is sealed off. We think he took special precautions to keep the computer area clean."

Morty nodded cautiously, hoping he was right. "How long does the organism take to work?"

"A few hours to a couple of days," Mike said.

"Anyone come down with it here yet?"

"No. Like I said, we're hoping the computer lab's clean. So far it has been."

Morty eyed the kids and remembered his responsibility. For an instant he considered sending them to a nearby hotel, but unless he found the cure they had little hope anyway.

"Well, Michael, lead on."

The lobby was small, a sofa, a couple of chairs with a phone between them, plants in the corners. A second agent, much taller than the first, greeted them with a stern handshake and darkly cool, suspicious eyes. "Agent Winfield Brost," he said, extending one hand. The other cradled a caramel-colored cat.

Kelly cooed and petted it as the introductions proceeded. "Agent Brost, this is Morty, Tim, and Kelly Craft."

"Why the kids?" Brost was direct.

"My assistants," Morty replied, leaving no room for argument.

Brost nodded, unconvinced.

"Why the cat?" Mike said with a tense edge.

"Came in this morning. I like cats." Brost sounded defiant, and Mike let the issue drop.

The computer room was a computer room in every sense of the word. About thirty feet square, there were shelves of documentation, no windows, and the far wall was crammed with gear.

"What is all this equipment?" Mike asked, as if he'd been

waiting for the opportunity to ask Morty since he'd first seen it two days ago.

"It's a computing arsenal. That's a Convex Minisuper-computer. Cruises about forty million instructions per second, or MIPS," Morty explained as he pointed to a beige, six-foot box whining in the corner. "Next to it we have a Silicon Graphics workstation." A multicolored screen saver danced magically across the TV-sized display. "It'll do some powerful imaging. That little box on top means it's 3D. Next to that we have an IBM RS6000. Very powerful workstation—40 to 60 MIPS."

Morty was clearly impressed. "Hmm. That next box is a WAVETRACER massively parallel system. I've only read about them. Brand-new design. He must be storing a lot of data because that knee-high box next to that is an EPOCH file server—that's where data is stored to feed the other computers."

Morty waved a hand toward a floor-to-ceiling rack in which four additional pieces of equipment were mounted. "I haven't the slightest idea what those are. You know—when you tie all this into the supercomputers down the street you've got yourself a pretty impressive setup."

"Sure makes for lots of cables," Tim observed. It did. Cables of all thicknesses snaked from device to device around the room's perimeter. The only thing they didn't seem to connect to was a desk strewn with piles of paper.

"He's serious." Kelly's eyes were huge. When she and Tim had put Morty's computer system together Tim had gotten excited about getting all the different components to work as a system. Her interest, however, was a little different. *I wonder how he's using all this,* she found herself thinking.

Morty picked up a pair of glasses that looked like binoculars with ear pieces. "These work with the Silicon Graphics workstation to make it 3D," Morty explained. "They give you a stereo effect by alternating your ability to see out of each eye and synchronize it with the display's stereo images. It's pretty cool." He set the glasses down.

Tim could do nothing but stare. He wanted to ask so many

questions and try so many things, yet he had no idea where to begin.

"Well, time to get to work." Morty sat down at the RS6000 and fired it up. He grabbed the mouse and selected a window on the screen. The window lit, and he typed in a couple of commands.

"What are you doing?" Mike asked.

"Looking at the file systems," Morty responded, his deft fingers never missing a beat as they clicked across the keyboard. "These boxes use UNIX as the operating system, and, except for the Cray Supercomputers, the file systems are primitive. I'd be surprised if we found anything here, but we have to look."

"Why won't you find anything?" Mike challenged.

"Helbert's smart. Unless he's hidden it in plain sight—like on that desk in all that paper—he's probably not going to hide it in a file system."

"We already searched all the paper. Nothing," Mike said.

Morty turned to Tim and Kelly. "Kids, go through the paper on the desk and see what you can find. I'll work here."

"I said we already went through all that," Mike repeated impatiently.

"They'll have a different perspective," Morty said.

So while Morty attacked the computers, Kelly and Tim attacked the desk.

After a few minutes the phone rang. Mike got it. "Agent Dunhill. . . . Yes, sir, they're at work. . . . Nothing yet. . . . But we've only been here an hour. . . . I'm aware of that, sir." He hung up.

Morty looked up and asked, "Your boss?"

Mike nodded. "Sort of. He's West Coast—Brost's and Howard's boss. We won't see him here."

Morty returned to work.

Another hour passed before Morty leaned back and rubbed tired eyes. He'd scanned all the files he could find—even written some simple programs to look for key words. Massively parallel systems were still very researchy and hard to use. It was possible that the information was hidden in one of the "black boxes" Morty didn't recognize, but they looked more like special purpose computers than data storage units. No. Matthew hadn't hidden his information here.

"What do you think, kids?" Morty finally asked. Kelly and Tim had finished their search about a half hour earlier and since then had been patiently waiting. Although Morty had asked the question rhetorically, Tim surprised him.

"We think there's more to this place," he said.

Morty's brows perked. "Why?"

Kelly said, "He was really into that recombinant DNA stuff. There's no doubt about that. Half the paper on this desk refers to that . . . "

"But?" Morty injected.

Kelly went on, "But the other half . . ."

Tim interrupted, "What's virtual reality?" He tossed Morty an article.

Morty read the title, "'How Real Can Virtual Reality Be?'"

"There's at least fifty articles like that," Kelly said. "Some he's written himself."

"What is it, Uncle Morty?" Tim asked.

Mike leaned forward, all ears.

"I guess you could call it the ultimate simulation." Morty glanced around the room but not finding what he wanted, gave a frustrated sigh and asked, "Tim, how do you know I'm here?"

"Huh?"

"How do you know that I'm here?"

"Well, I see you. I hear you talking to me . . . "

"You see me in relationship to the room," Morty added. "I behave as you expect. I don't walk through walls, and so forth. That's reality."

"Right."

"Now, what if a helmet kept you from seeing the outside world and on the inside presented you with an animated graphic of me sitting here talking, a graphic where I did what you expected and didn't walk through walls? That would look like reality, but it wouldn't be. It would be simulated reality, or 'virtual reality.'"

Kelly asked, "What's it used for?"

"Well, there's not only a helmet to feed you images, but gloves that give you virtual feel. Here." He tossed her a pen he'd been using.

After holding the pen in her hand for a moment, she said, "I see. The gloves make you think you're feeling it. Like I feel the pen."

"So with the helmet, the gloves, and a fast enough computer to feed the appropriate images and senses, you can use it to teach things. I've heard people talk about using it to teach surgeons. You could feed them the images of the person's anatomy and the feeling of holding the scalpel, cutting, and suturing."

"I'd die. I hate blood." Kelly winced.

"The key to virtual reality is a very fast computer and a way for it to accept and transmit lots of information."

Kelly said, "Would any of these computers be fast enough?"

Morty looked around as if to confirm what he already knew. "No. I don't think so." But he saw that Kelly had more to say. "What are you thinking?" he asked.

"You know two things well," she began, "art and computers. If you were trying to hide something from someone who knew computers, where would you hide it?"

"I'd paint it in blue on my barn—what's left of my barn."

"And if you were hiding it from someone who knew art."

Morty didn't hesitate. "In the computer. I see your point. If he's trying to hide it from someone who knows biochem he'd hide it in the computer—in virtual reality. But I'm not sure technology's capable of doing such a thing. Or at least any kind of virtual reality complex enough to hide something in it."

"But he's a genius, Uncle Morty," Kelly insisted. "And if he does have a virtual reality machine he's got it somewhere else."

Morty couldn't deny that point, but both Tim and Kelly knew he wasn't convinced. Eager to get on to something productive, Morty said, "I want to ask some friends if they can find the formula in the data here, and then we'll talk some more."

Mike asked, "What friends?"

"Friends." A small book appeared from Morty's back pocket, and he thumbed through it until he found the page he wanted. He grabbed a phone and punched in eleven numbers. It rang and someone answered. "Aging Rookie," Morty said and he waited. "Golden Bits," he said.

The voice at the other end said something.

"I've got a priority code search here. I'm going to send you about ten gigabytes of data. Run it through, and tell me what you find."

The voice crackled again.

"Both 64 and 32 bit. But that shouldn't matter much. Crunch it and give me a call back. I'll use my usual line."

Morty hung up.

Mike nodded his approval. "I should have thought of that."

"That's why I get paid the big bucks."

"Who was that?" Tim asked.

"Can't say. But he has computer power coming out his ears and his big thing is breaking codes. We'll let him work on this data for a while." Within ten minutes the computers and workstations were dumping their data over satellites to the secret location.

Tim spoke, "You don't buy the virtual reality thing, do you, Uncle Morty?"

"Every potential solution has to be logical, Tim. I don't think that technology's progressed far enough for him to use it that way. My guess is he's very interested in the concept, and he might actually be using the 3D display here to do some experiments, but . . ."

Kelly interrupted, "I still say he's a genius, and geniuses can do things that normal people . . ."

"I'm a genius, too, Kelly, and the one thing a genius learns is that he's bound by technology and, ultimately, logic."

That's when logic took a leap toward fantasy. Tim, feeling the same sense of defeat as Kelly, leaned hard against the documentation bookcase. Suddenly a motor whirred, and the bookcase fell back a notch and slid away. Tim caught his balance before he fell and the others turned. "A room," Mike whispered.

"What's that, Uncle Morty?" Kelly exclaimed as she pointed.

A small gray box sat in the corner. Octagonal, it stood about three feet high and had a series of three red buttons on top. It was connected to two cables which attached to what looked like deep sea diving suits. They hung on the wall, one on either side of the gray box. Topped by helmets, the suits themselves were black and made of material stiff enough to hold much of their shape as they hung. The gloves and boots were ribbed with thin metal strips.

About six feet in front of the box, about as far apart, were two stages, each about six inches high and two feet square, each with places to strap boots at their center. In the corner near the door stood a tall, steel, bullet-shaped cylinder. Painted down the side in haphazard lettering was the word "Digitizer." A thick black cable led from the digitizer to the octagonal box, and above the box hung a large screen. Next to the door was a small desk, chair, and a keyboard. The room was tomb quiet.

Morty stood still—first surprised, then, very slowly, his surprise dissolved to admiration.

"He did it," Morty whispered to the silent room. "I'll be. He beat me good this time."

CHAPTER 5

The infectious disease ward was a fortress of glass. Thick panes of it surrounded patients, nurses, and the corridor. A negative pressure air-conditioning system kept dust and human breath inside when the door was opened. An antiseptic odor permeated the entire area.

Tanya Walsh, at fourteen, was a slight girl with short, disheveled wheat-brown hair and hollow, blue eyes. Those eyes gave her an anxiously tentative look. The fact that her mother lay on the other side of the glass, unconscious and hooked up to a wall of monitors, didn't decrease that anxiety at all.

Sitting in a vinyl chair, she watched her mother's doctor enter. He was of average height, average build, average face, and wore a white smock. But it wouldn't have mattered if he was wearing a clown suit and red shock-wig; none of it would have registered. He was just there to make her mother well again—that's what mattered.

His black name tag read Dr. Call. He was her mother's doctor because he seemed to be everyone's doctor in intensive care. He was monitoring at least four other unconscious patients. "You're Maddie Walsh's daughter?" he asked.

"How is she doing, Dr. Call?" Tanya asked, trying to sound confident.

"Holding her own."

"Can you believe this happened on her birthday?" Tanya fought back a tear with a worried little laugh. "We own a diner on the coast highway. We were going to do something special when her replacement came—but she just collapsed on the floor."

"It must have been horrible," Dr. Call said with what sounded like true sympathy.

"Can I go in and sit with her? This seems so far away," Tanya said.

"No. We don't want you getting it."

"What did the tests say?"

"Nothing yet," Dr. Call said. "We've done some local tests, but we've sent them all down to Scripps in San Diego. If anyone can find it, those people can."

Tanya nodded. "Will she die?" she asked, pain harnessed in her voice.

"Not if I have anything to say about it."

"Do you have anything to say about it?" Tanya asked.

Dr. Call smiled compassionately down at her. "Want to join me for a Coke down in the cafeteria? My treat."

"No. I don't want to miss it if she wakes up."

Dr. Call patted her shoulder. "I'll be back soon. If she wakes, push the button—" he pointed to a buzzer on the sill marked 'For Nursing Assistance' "—and tell the nurse."

"Okay. Do you think she might wake up?" Tanya asked and turned back to the window and her mother.

"If she does, I want you to be the first to know."

Tanya again laughed nervously. "I'll go for that."

Feeling near reverence, Morty approached the octagonal box. Without hesitation he pressed the red "Load" button on top. The box woke with a surge of electric whirring, and the screen above the box lit. Canted slightly downward, the screen could be easily seen from anywhere in the room. It said:

Welcome to Helbertland
Name(s), Please

"When did Matthew get a sense of humor?" Morty asked whoever was listening.

"I'll type it in," Tim said, stepping quickly to the keyboard.

"Enter my name," Morty instructed.

"What about us?" Kelly asked, her voice laced with disappointment.

"Matthew can be unpredictable. I'll fly solo for the time being until we know a little more."

Tim didn't like it either, but he did as he was told. He typed "Morty Craft," and it appeared on the screen.

From behind the screen came a voice. Although electronically constructed, it possessed real inflection and the slight imperfections that separate reality from imitation. It said, "Welcome, Morty. Are there others?"

Before Tim could type, Morty answered, "Just me."

"Fine," said the voice. "You must be digitized."

"I must?" asked Morty. Kelly noticed he was avoiding "yes" and "no" to see how extensive the computer's vocabulary and syntax were. So far it was doing pretty well.

"Yes. Go to the digitizer in the corner, please. Press the blue button, then step inside. And remember, smile and the whole world smiles with you."

Morty's brows furled. *No smiles from him*, Kelly thought as he did as he was told. The moment the button was pushed, a crack the length of the cylinder appeared that widened to a door. With a hesitant glance at everyone in the room, Morty stepped inside and the door closed.

Kelly eyed Tim, and they both looked at Mike as a hydraulic sound came from the cylinder. Something was moving inside.

"What's going on?" Mike asked.

"It's digitizing him. I think it's turning what he looks like into something the computer can understand—a series of bits," Tim explained.

"The bit is the smallest amount of information a computer has. It's either zero or one. Eight bits is a byte," Kelly explained. "You can make 256 different characters or codes with eight bits arranged in zeros and ones."

Mike nodded. But he didn't really care.

"I've heard of digitizing pictures and pages of words, but

this is weird," Tim said as the hydraulic sound ended and the door to the cylinder slid open.

Morty emerged, rubbing his eyes. "That's quite a piece of equipment. I wonder when he had time to do biochem. Putting that thing together had to be a full-time job."

"Morty," the voice from behind the screen called, "please put on your entry suit."

"Which one?"

"It doesn't matter. I know you now."

Morty looked at the kids. "Sounds ominous."

Before Morty stepped into the suit, he examined it carefully. Although as light as tissue paper, its skin was reasonably rigid and stood at least six feet, six inches tall. The helmet looked like a plastic bubble with no eyeholes and would definitely close inside whoever wore it. The zipper in front slid down easily, and with the suit now open, Morty examined the inside.

The inside front of the helmet was light blue while the back was as black at the outside. The inside body was laced with a tight mesh of thin wires with a loose mesh of thicker wires superimposed on top of them. The wires gave the suit its rigidity.

Morty crammed his feet into the boots, and the moment his feet rested on the soles, the sides and tops of the boots swelled around the contour of his foot. The rest of the suit hung loosely on him. The voice said, "Before you don the helmet, strap the boots to the appropriate place on one of the stages."

Morty stepped to the stage nearest him and placed his feet in the boot-sized depressions. The straps manipulated easily.

"Put on the helmet and zip up the suit," the voice instructed further.

With the kids' help, Morty was quickly cocooned inside. Tim and Kelly stepped back and smiled at each other. Morty looked strange—like a black-suited moon walker.

Morty began to walk, or at least that's how it looked to everyone outside. The stage remained stationary, but the top rose and fell with footsteps. His hands swung normally, head moving from side to side as if surveying his surroundings. Then an arm lifted and a finger jutted out and pressed something. He ducked slightly, took a couple of steps, then straightened and walked some more.

"This is spooky," Tim whispered.

"He went into something," Kelly observed, eyes glued on her uncle.

"What's going on?" Mike looked dumbfounded.

"He must be seeing things and reacting to them," Tim answered.

Morty's pace changed. It became more leisurely, and his head bobbed and turned as if talking to people, then he'd wave and go on to someone else. After a few minutes he leaned slightly forward, his steps becoming more labored, as if walking uphill.

"He looks silly!" Kelly laughed. He did—in his black suit, standing on a box, walking nowhere, head and arms bobbing in silent reaction to imaginary events. "Just plain silly. If I go in there all of you will have to leave the room."

Morty began to look even sillier. He stopped, greeted someone with an elaborate bow, then, after a moment's talk, extended his arm as if to a lady at a ball. Then he began to skip!

Kelly blushed for her uncle and turned to see Mike and Tim folded with laughter.

"I wish I had my camcorder. I'd send it to 'Funniest Home Videos,'" Mike said, shaking with laughter.

The door to the lab opened, and the taller of the two agents, Brost, stepped in, the tabby cat still cradled on his arm. "What's going on?" he asked.

"Who knows?" Mike called back to him as Brost caught sight of the black suit skipping. His expression was first surprise, then disbelief. "What's that?"

"Virtual reality," Tim explained. "Makes you wonder, doesn't it?"

"Yeah," said Brost.

Morty's skipping evolved into something else. "He's hopping!" Kelly couldn't believe her eyes. "Like a bunny." No mistaking it. He crouched, his arms up, hands bent out beneath his chin, and he hopped.

"Like a bunny, huh?" Brost winced, and the cat, too, shook its head as if in disbelief. Brost turned to Mike. "It's spreading."

Mike sobered. "How many more?"

"Seventeen," Brost said, "and the lid's off. The media's got hold of it. The Bureau's speculating that more may have collapsed that we don't know about. Maybe hundreds. They're trying to keep the lab a secret. Who knows if we'll succeed?"

Mike saw him glance at Morty again. "Believe it or not we may be onto something here," Mike told him.

"Looks like it," Brost said dryly. "We got the preliminary report of ChemTech, privately owned by Hammond Helbert."

"That fits."

"And Helbert owns a private jet."

"A Paris IIB?"

"You got it." Brost handed him a couple of sheets of paper, which Mike scanned quickly.

"Thanks," Mike said.

Brost nodded vaguely, then asked, "You guys want a Coke or anything?"

"Yes, thanks," Kelly said. Tim agreed.

"Coffee," Mike said. A few minutes later Brost returned with the drinks.

"Where's your cat?" Kelly asked.

"He's having his coffee outside," Brost responded taking a long look at Morty. But while the others sipped their drinks and giggled at his antics, Brost remained sober. Finally he said, "Don't forget people could die from this."

Mike eyed him with strong resentment. "We won't."

Feeling the reprimand, Brost left.

"I didn't know he was in such good shape," Kelly said as Morty began to duck walk.

Suddenly Morty stood, rigidly tense. Something had changed. His right hand flew up and grasped something— something with weight. Morty swung it. Then he dipped and dodged, spun around and swung it again . . .

"A sword fight?" Tim asked, the question woven with concern.

It looked like one. The black suit dodged an invisible onslaught, jumped to the side and dipped, and swung. The top of Morty's box was alive as the "battle" raged. Morty dropped to one knee, his arms erect, fending off a particularly hard blow. Then he maneuvered back to his feet and swung the "sword" again and again at his attacker. The attacker seemed to swing back, and Morty sucked his middle in to avoid the "blade."

"I don't like this," Kelly said, eyes riveted on the "combat."

"I wonder what he sees," Mike asked, his coffee forgotten.

"How real is it?" Tim asked. "Can it hurt him?"

As if to give an immediate answer, Morty dodged a "blow" and immediately grabbed and massaged his right arm above the elbow.

"He's hit!" Tim gasped.

"He's in pain." Kelly felt it with him.

"Should we stop it?" Mike asked.

"How?" Kelly asked. "And what if we did? Maybe he couldn't get out of the suit!" Kelly stepped forward, so close that when Morty straightened and swung his injured arm, he nearly hit her.

Tim pulled her back.

Morty was up again. His arm was sluggish, and obviously injured, but he fought on. And as he did, his movements slowed and became more plodding. He was beginning to tire.

Kelly frowned. "Do you think he can die?"

Suddenly Morty planted himself defensively on one knee. With his weapon held with both hands above his head, his body repeatedly shuddered as his weapon absorbed blow after blow from his unseen enemy.

Driven toward the earth, the pounding weakening him, Morty was about to collapse when something happened. A spark of energy returned and he looked to his left—to the sky. His enemy must have left, for after a moment or two, Morty painfully stood. He'd only been on his feet for a second when he stiffened again and dove, but he never reached the ground. The suit stiffened and suspended him at about a forty-five-degree angle, arms extended and folded over his head. If on the ground, he would have been protecting the back of his head while his face was pushed into the dirt.

There was a sudden jolt. His body lifted violently, then relaxed. Morty's left hand came down and pushed the palm of his right glove. Immediately, the suit rose to an upright position. Weary and beaten, Morty unzipped the suit. The voice returned from behind the screen. "Come again," it said. "We enjoyed having you."

CHAPTER 6

U ncle Morty looked exhausted, but smiled broadly the moment he saw the others.

"What a ride!" he said, his breath forced from bruised ribs. He massaged his right arm.

"Are you hurt?" Kelly sprang up, her arm around him, holding him steady.

Tim, too, was by his other side giving support.

"I'm okay, really. I just feel hurt. Weirdest contraption I ever . . . Disneyland ought to install this thing."

"What happened?" Mike asked, trying to get back to the important issue.

Morty saw Mike's Styrofoam cup. "Coffee? Would one of you guys get me a cup?"

Tim nodded and ran out and quickly returned with a steaming cup.

"Thank you." Morty took a sip. "Okay, where to begin? First, it feels real. You hear sounds and see things and feel things," he said as he rubbed his arm. "Sometimes pain. When your head moves, things appear stationary. That's a real breakthrough in virtual reality's development. Matthew's done it. The smells are a little vague, but at times they work."

"The formula?" Mike reminded him of his mission.

Kelly added, "It's an epidemic now. People are dropping like flies out there."

Morty nodded. "Still no clues. But from the looks of it Matthew's set this thing up as an Alice-in-Wonderland-type place, medieval, with a series of tests. It's consistent with his competitive personality. Maybe if you pass the tests . . . ? At first I went through a town—English from the accents—old cobbled streets. A big old church. Beggars. All the trappings. One slight difference: the townspeople were chess pieces.

"Knights on horse's heads, bishops with little knobby faces, pawns everywhere. A king and queen crossed the street in front of me. I felt like I was watching a cartoon." Morty smiled and went on, "I guess I was. Anyway, the pieces greeted me, talked about the weather, one challenged me to a game of chess. I refused. I could see me getting bogged down for hours. Then they let me know that if I was going on beyond the town I needed to . . . how'd they say it? Yes, 'beat a beautiful lass at her own game.'"

"Chess?" Kelly asked.

"Her game, as best I can describe it, was cavorting. I met her at the other end of town and she was beautiful." For an instant Morty relived the look of her, and Kelly felt almost embarrassed. "Big, warm eyes . . . "

"Uncle Morty!" Kelly scolded.

"When's my turn?" Mike grinned.

"You can't." Morty laughed. "You're married."

"You hopped?" Tim brought Morty back.

"And duck walked," Morty went on. "She had this list of things I had to do."

Morty paused. "I think the program knows all—respiration, heart rate, tension. It knew I was getting tired. Maybe that's what it was doing. I was being worn out—very pleasantly—but worn out, nonetheless."

"And then a knight came?" Tim conjectured.

"I guess that's what he was," Morty said, taking another sip of coffee. "If knights wear business suits."

"Business suits?" Mike asked.

"Right off Pennsylvania Avenue—with a hat and briefcase. And he challenged me to a fight." Morty massaged his arm again. "Since I'd passed on the chess game I figured I needed to accept this challenge in order to make a step toward the formula. But I immediately wished I'd passed.

"The moment I accepted he became a knight—with armor

and everything. Then I realized I had a sword in my hand and we went at it. MIT was not big on swordplay. He beat me up pretty bad."

"You fought hard," Kelly said with deep admiration. "We watched from out here."

"You could see what I saw?" Morty asked surprised.

"No, just you and the suit. But the battle was obvious," she answered.

"Not everything was obvious," Tim added. "How did it end? The knight seemed to disappear, and then you dove for cover."

"An F-something-or-other swooped out of the sky, planted a few rounds on a nearby hill and scared him. He ran away. I thought things were turning to the better when the fighter turned its guns on me. A couple of rounds landed a few yards away. I dove for the dirt, protected myself and when the thunder ended I decided I'd had enough for the moment."

"You pressed your right palm," Tim observed.

"That's how you get out of the suit—either the right or the left. This thing is incredible. The graphics are first-rate, the interaction flawless. I don't know how fast the computer in that little box is, but it has to be phenomenal."

"It brings up your question again. How did he have time to create both this and the coma bug?" Mike mused.

"You think ChemTech might have helped him out?" Morty asked. "Have you gotten your report yet?"

Mike nodded. "Hammond Helbert owns ChemTech."

Morty wasn't surprised. "We had a feeling he was involved in this some way. I didn't know he was into biochemistry, though."

Mike went on, "He was the one in the jet too."

"Busy guy," Morty said.

"Something else," Mike added. "Matthew Helbert hated chess. He found it as boring as watching paint dry. Hammond loved it though. He was state chess champ and could have gone higher if he'd had the time."

"He had a passion for English history, too, didn't he?" Morty pointed out.

"Read it and lived it. He belonged to one of those medieval clubs. They had tournaments—jousts and things," Mike confirmed. "Do you think Matthew's little wonderland here is set up for Hammond?" he continued.

"Maybe to trap him? They hated each other," Morty said. "To team up together they would both need an incredible reason."

"Maybe the partnership soured," Tim suggested.

"It'd be nice to know," Mike said abruptly, "but how we got here isn't as important as finding our way out. Morty, ole boy, you've got to get back into Helbert's wonderland and find that formula."

"I wonder if the East Coast has discovered anything in that data yet. Any word from them?" Morty asked.

"No," Mike said and stepped toward the front door. "I'll get Northern California working on Hammond. Maybe we can find him. It's a cinch he knows more than we do right now."

Morty nodded and eyed the suit again. When Mike left, the kids stepped closer to Morty.

"If this guy's brother tried to shake us up getting here . . . " Kelly began.

"How dangerous do you think it is in there?" Tim asked.

"If you're thinking he could get in there with me, there are only two suits, and we know where both of them are," Morty said calmly. He rubbed his arm and went on, "Anyway, it's all virtual pain, isn't it? But, dangerous or not, the Lord's given us the opportunity to help. We have to go forward."

"Like Joseph on the throne of Egypt? God put him there for a reason—I guess we're here for a reason too," Kelly said.

"Just like Joseph," Morty affirmed and moved toward the suit and stepped back into it. When the zipper was up the voice said, "Name, please."

"Morty Craft," Morty replied as he slipped the helmet on and felt it close snugly under his chin.

"Welcome back, Morty Craft," the voice said as the blackness within the helmet dissolved to now familiar images.

Morty lay in the dirt again, the faint rumble of a jet fighter fading in the distance.

He didn't know it, but eyes were watching him, eyes that had seen his battle with the knight, seen the jet attack him, and seen him disappear and now reappear. The same eyes would continue to watch where he went and what he found.

Morty got to his feet; his upper arm hurt as it had before, the faint, bitter smell of explosive stung his nostrils, and he was sure he felt the aftershock from the round that hit closest to him.

Morty looked ahead.

A hill rolled up to the left of him, but ahead and to the right the earth sprawled flat and brown—lifeless—a near desert. He could feel he was being given a choice: either step out over the harsh terrain, or return to the village—maybe to meet the beautiful English lass again. He felt a smile creep across his lips. He could handle that.

The town it was. Maybe playing chess with the inhabitants would matter. He spun around.

And his nose pressed against a closed, wooden door. He stepped back, looked right, then left. The door was part of a long, high, brick wall that stretched forever in either direction. He pushed the door—solid as stone. He tried the ancient brass handle. It jiggled, but did little else.

He surveyed the full expanse of the wall again. Computer graphics can reach to eternity, and this one did. Not only did the wall continue in both directions until it faded to the horizon, but it reached to the sky.

It was obvious that he'd not be going back to town.

Morty took another step back to see if he'd missed any features of the wall; as he did a deep shadow fell over him. He spun around.

The desert had vanished and a dense, thorny thicket had replaced it. The tangled branches blocked the sun and sent a shadowy mesh closing over him. But it wasn't the shadows or the thicket's endless sprawl that he found frightening. It was the thorns. They were immense and sharp—like giant fangs, or swords. They were borne on intertwined branches, and they dueled with one another in a growing breeze.

Morty saw one saving grace: the thicket hovered at least ten feet off the ground. Held aloft by thick, woven tree trunks that sprang up at wide intervals, it stood high enough for him to walk easily under it. It would actually provide needed shade and make traveling easier.

But after his first few steps under it, things changed.

At first, Morty noticed just a curious lightness in his step.

Then he became truly weightless—as if helium filled, like a float in a parade. The ground became something to reach for, and the thorns, only seconds before curious oddities, now loomed above him like deadly spikes.

CHAPTER 7

During a brief stint at Johnson Space Center in Houston, Morty had experienced weightlessness. Gravity seemed to be one of those things appreciated only when absent. No longer was everything pulled toward Earth. At the space center, Morty's feet no longer bore his weight, his hands no longer felt heavy, even his insides no longer piled on top of one another. They floated. The reorientation was dramatic. He could literally swim through air. Although VR wasn't able to simulate true weightlessness, it added another ingredient of its own—terror—as he rose to meet the thorns.

Each thorn was well over a foot long and sharpened to a needle point, and everywhere Morty looked he saw tangles of them. Some were straight as arrows, others twisted and bent, still others curved gracefully. No matter what their shape, like a school of hungry sharks, they were all poised and waiting.

He reached up with one hand and grabbed the lowest branch he could find, then grabbed the end of a thorn with the other hand and tried to steady himself. But his back end floated up and a thorn stabbed his leg. The wound burned deeply, and he recoiled, kicking the injured leg toward earth.

Now he saw something else. A coconut was growing from a nearby branch. Knowing it would be easier to hang onto than a sharp thorn, Morty grabbed it. It broke free from the branch.

Unexpectedly, his hand fell under its weight. Morty considered this for a moment. Maybe with a couple more he could weigh himself down. As a nearby thorn, jostled by wind, stung his arm, he ripped another coconut off. Now that hand went down—not very far, but enough to force the other end of him higher. Again, his leg struck a thorn, and again the electric shock of it rifled through him.

But now he knew. If he could distribute the coconuts all over his body, he'd be able to weigh himself down.

Sparring with the thorns, he continued to gather coconuts. The first few he dropped to earth to be retrieved later. But he quickly realized that wouldn't work—he needed the coconuts to get down there. Finding a small hammock of tangled branches he stacked them there. When he had ten he faced the next challenge.

Getting them onto his body.

He noticed that he was wearing the sport shirt and slacks he'd traveled in and remembered that the computer had digitized him in his clothes before he had donned the black suit. There was no way he could stuff the coconuts into his clothes and still button things up. He had to find another way.

Bobbing beneath the thicket he peered deeply into it.

He saw nothing but thick branches, jutting thorns, and distant sprinkles of light. Then he noticed the vines. Morty grabbed one and pulled. It remained firm. As a helium filled balloon he had little leverage and tugging accomplished nothing. So he spun around and planted his feet on a branch, grabbed the vine, and, using leg and arm muscles, pulled again. The vine gave—too quickly. Suddenly propelled by the power in his legs, Morty spun about erratically so that he had no way of protecting himself.

But someone else must have been protecting him, because he slammed into a limb, safely wedged between two saber-sharp thorns.

He wasn't sure whether to thank God or Matthew's programming. Making the obvious choice, he whispered, "Thanks, Lord," a sense of relief washing over him.

He studied the vine closely. It was just as he'd hoped. The thicker vine was really just a tightly twisted pack of thinner vines—like a rope. Working branch by branch, he returned to his coconut cache and quickly went to work. Spreading the smaller strands of vine apart, he slipped a coconut in the middle of them. As he had hoped, the vines closed around it and held it fast. He did another and another until he had a ten-foot rope of coconuts. Draping it over his shoulders, he lashed either end of the vine to his legs. Then he let go of the branches he'd used to steady himself.

He dropped like a rock—so hard, in fact, that he hurt his backside.

After nursing his bruise for a moment, he tried to get up. He couldn't. A moment ago he was weightless, now he had anvils in his pockets. But he knew the coconuts weren't that heavy. "Matthew's playing games," Morty growled as he untied the vines from his legs. Suddenly weightless again, his legs shot straight up. Did Matthew want him to walk on his hands?

Not sure what to do next, Morty found himself grabbing the coconuts on either end of the chain and to his surprise, his legs immediately settled gently to the ground. He still felt light, but now he stood upright. He'd found a way through the thorns—it had been a test and he'd passed—a riddle and he'd solved it. To continue he had to hold the coconuts, one in each hand.

Maybe things were going to be easy now.

Although the thicket overhead shrouded the ground in dark shadows, he distinguished a narrow path through the thick, forest-bed soil. It meandered a bit, but he decided to follow it anyway.

Now that the immediate danger had passed, Morty allowed his senses to rest—he took a moment to absorb the world around him. Below, the earth shuffled gently beneath his shoes. Now and then a distant bird chirped. If the thicket weren't so bizarre, his walk would be as refreshing as an early morning stroll in the woods near his farm.

The thought of his farm brought a chuckle.

Although at one time it had been a farm, it wasn't one now and probably never would be again. He knew nothing about farming. His brother, John, was the farmer—a good farmer. More than that, John was a good man; a man in tune with everything around him—wife, kids, God, work, world. Morty had envied him.

In the bureaucratic jungle of Washington, working on one secret project after another, Morty had suddenly felt distant from God—so far from what it seemed God might want for him that he decided to pack up and leave. Maybe living near John, a man who had not only taken hold of God's purpose but had built a wonderful family and farm with it, Morty would find his own purpose.

But that search would have to wait for now. This one was far more important. And here, beneath thorns and branches and coconuts, he had never felt further from either goal.

He suddenly heard footsteps.

He spun around, eyes sweeping the shadows. No movement—and the only things standing were the thick, twisted trunks that held up the thicket—nothing else. Someone could be behind one of them, but Morty couldn't see him.

He turned back and his heart leaped to his throat.

A snake—its mouth gaping, its teeth every bit as menacing as the thorns, hung inches from his nose.

With a horrified gasp, Morty fell several steps back.

Eyes riveting, its tongue flicking incessantly, the snake's sleek body grew longer and reached further down from the thicket above.

Morty stepped further back, but the snake stalked him, its yellow eyes haunting Morty.

"Hello," hissed the snake, its voice unwinding from the very tip of its tail.

"Hello," managed Morty.

"Welcome to my thicket," it said, more air than sound.

"Will we be fighting?" Morty asked.

The snake laughed an airy laugh. "I never fight my guests," it said.

"Why don't I trust you?"

This laugh sent the corners of its mouth to its ear holes. "Perhaps you were the victim of bad parenting," the snake speculated.

Morty stepped back again, but the yellow eyes and the wide, grinning mouth closed the gap again.

"Then back off," Morty said firmly.

"You misjudge me," said the snake. "I'm such a gentle creature." It smiled a smile that Morty could picture on the snake in Eden.

That was it. Morty saw no use waiting for the inevitable attack. Taking the offensive, he swung both coconuts with the intent of smashing the snake's head between them. But the creature bolted, and the coconuts cracked together harmlessly.

"Now that wasn't neighborly," the snake said, its smile gone. Now the eyes blazed, and the head slithered forward.

Realizing that the coconut chain would make a powerful weapon, Morty removed it from his shoulders, but the moment he did his body rose. Feeling infinitely vulnerable, he looped the chain back over his neck and as he settled back to earth, swung a coconut in his hand. He missed.

"Oops!" The snake was mocking him now.

"You're not real," Morty pointed out.

"Oh?" said the snake and his head lunged at Morty. The cavernous mouth, lined with sharp teeth, snapped a breadth from Morty's nose. Morty swung the rock-hard coconut again.

"I'm through playing," the snake cooed. To prove the point it snapped again, then again. Morty swung the coconuts, missing each time. He knew that in seconds the slithering body would be around his own. In desperation, he swung once more.

Suddenly he heard a pulsing whine in the air. Just as suddenly something hit the snake and sliced the head from its body. The headless serpent writhed and contorted. When death overtook it, the thick body hung limply from the thicket. After a moment its tail lost its grip, and the body fell wholly to earth.

With heart pounding, glad he was still alive, Morty turned to see from where his help had come.

Nothing stirred. Someone had saved him—or maybe Matthew's programming had. But either way, no one rose to take credit. Not far from the lifeless head lay the bloody weapon—a split thorn that had grown slightly curved. Someone had picked it, split it down the middle, and created a very sharp sword.

He looked around again.

If a friend had done it, why didn't he show himself?

If an enemy, why had he saved him?

Morty scanned the area for a final time, then eyed the snake's severed head. "Are there more like you around here?"

The snake didn't answer.

CHAPTER 8

The coconut chain draped over his neck, the two ends secure in his hands, Morty continued on. After only a few steps he heard footsteps again. When he turned, though, he saw no one. He stood peering into the shadows for several seconds. He had the distinct feeling he was being watched.

Maybe it was his imagination. It certainly had enough to work with: the unearthly shadows, the constant rattling of thorns overhead, the possibility of another snake. Although his brain reminded him that he was trekking through a computer never-never land, his arms and legs still hurt from where they'd been "stabbed" via electric shock by thorns. There was enough reality here to keep his attention—especially when he began to notice the distance between the ground and his thorny sky diminishing. The thicket was closing in.

As it turned out, what he'd thought was a distant horizon turned out to be a narrow opening. Hands still filled with the coconuts, he stooped, then crawled, and before long he was maneuvering on his stomach, wiggling past one thorn at a time. Fortunately, there were no more snakes, and he finally emerged from the menacing thicket to blue sky and green, dandelion-speckled meadows. A constant breeze bent the grass in picturesque waves.

He stood for a moment to savor the sudden beauty and to praise God for his keeping through the thorns when a woman screamed. First only a faint prick of sound in his ear, the sound gradually increased in volume. No mistaking the fear in the scream. Morty heard the shrieks again and again, each time sounding closer. He spun about. The thicket was still there. He spun again—the meadow stretched forever. He could see no one. Yet the noise was incessant, shrill, terror-struck. Morty's eyes darted left, then right. He took a few steps forward thinking he could get a different perspective. He didn't.

The screams grew even louder. The woman had to be running toward him. But where was she? The scene was still pastoral. The grass still waved, the wildflowers still danced in the sunlight—all unaffected by the approaching cries. She couldn't be more than ten yards away now and heading right at him.

He heard the faint thunder of hoofbeats. The sound was like a cattle stampede but further off, dulled by the meadow.

Suddenly the shrieks dulled to anxious breathing, and something grabbed Morty's arm. The instant he felt the touch a woman appeared—her hand on his wounded shoulder, her face a picture of anguish. It took him several heart-beats to recognize her. She was the beautiful English lass who had him duck-walking near the village. "Help me. He's after me!" she cried desperately.

"Who?"

"The dragon," she said, eyes huge, her face a terrified mask.

"Where? I can't see him."

"He's there. You need your sword." Still holding him, she ducked behind him and used him for a shield.

"Why can't I see him? I can't fight what I can't see."

"He's coming. Oh, Lord help me, he's coming." She released Morty and dashed toward the thicket. But the moment she let go, she disappeared.

"You're kidding," Morty gasped. "I have to fight a dragon, and the only time I can see it is when it's chewing on me?" He cried to the sky above, "You gotta be kidding, Matthew."

The sound of hooves grew louder.

"Please save me," the woman whimpered, a bit further

away, but close enough for him to know she was depending on him.

Morty turned toward the thicket. The thorns were low enough to be accessible, and swinging a branch of them in the direction of the dragon would cut a wide, deadly swath. Maybe there was a defense against this thing.

Instinctively he dropped the coconuts and grabbed for the nearest branch, but immediately he drifted upward.

"Where are you going?" her sniffling voice asked.

He grabbed the coconuts again. "Nowhere. I have to hold these coconuts or I float away."

"No," her panic returned, "you can't just drift away. You have to save me. He'll toast me, roast me, make a ghost of me."

"Poetry! Matthew Helbert loved poetry," Morty suddenly remembered. He couldn't write it worth beans, as he had just proved—but he loved it.

The thought of Matthew refreshed the fact that all this was no more than a lavish cartoon. Who cared if cartoons hurt one another? Morty felt a sudden urge to leave the woman to suffer a virtual death at the hands of a virtual dragon.

But then she said, "Please save me, I can help you find what you seek."

"You can?"

"Surely." Her hands grabbed him again, and she reappeared—eyes large, soft, peering deeply into his, hands warm and urgent.

Morty's heart pounded. "But I have a problem," he said. "The only weapon I have against the dragon is the thorns. To rip off a branch of them I have to drop the coconuts. But when I drop the coconuts I drift away."

"And?" the woman said, eyes still large.

"You have to help me. You have to tear out the thorny branch."

"Why?" She wasn't thrilled with the idea.

"Because I can't," Morty reaffirmed—just a little irritated.

The woman thought. "Hrumph," she grunted. "Coconuts drop and you drift off to the sun." She eyed the thicket, then spoke, "If I get the weapons then what good are you? Why should I take you where you want to go if I have to save myself?"

She has a point, Morty thought. "Okay, you win," he said. "Grab one end of the coconut chain and hold it so I don't fly off, and I'll get the weapon."

"Sounds good," she said grabbing the coconut he offered and holding it tightly. As it turned out she didn't disappear. Touching something he held must keep her visible.

Morty drifted up. Being on the end of the chain made him feel like a balloon in the Macy's Thanksgiving Day parade. The breeze took him toward the thicket, and he was able to yank off a branch after some effort.

What a weapon! It was an eight-foot string of thorns. As it turned out he was none too soon. His English lass screamed again, this time wailing that the dragon was only a few yards away.

Suddenly Morty heard a jet-like whine, and his leg ignited as if it had been hit by a blowtorch.

Writhing in agony, he kicked and spun and swung his lethal bat around. He struck something, and the dragon appeared. Slime green, eyes narrow with outrage, the dragon stood twenty feet tall, higher than Morty floated. Acrid gray smoke billowed from its nostrils, and its lips were black and scorched. Modeled after a Tyrannosaurus rex, it stood on its hind legs peering down at him with boiling eyes, while its small forelegs clawed at the air. It was in pain.

The thorns had done some damage. Needle sharp, they dug deeply into the reptilian skin; blood oozed from one wound and gushed from another. But in spite of the wounds, the creature was still very dangerous.

Morty pulled the whip of thorns back to prepare for another attack. The moment he did the dragon disappeared, but he had no doubt that it was still there. Morty immediately felt an explosion of fire hit his midsection, and the English lass screamed below him.

He swung the thorns blindly and felt them dig deeply into the dragon's flesh—it reappeared and confirmed the strike. This time the reptile blazed away on the thorny branch—under a puff of flame the branch became a harmless rope of ash. And Morty's hand was painfully blistered.

Again the dragon disappeared, and now Morty saw the grass where the dragon stood flatten. It was probably preparing to eat Morty whole.

He heard the woman below say, "Oh, yes. Please! Please!"

Morty looked down and saw a man. From his perch atop the coconut chain, Morty could only see the top of the man's balding head and an expanse of muscular shoulders. In his hand was a single, long, gracefully bent thorn.

Without reply, the man took off in a wide circle, stalking the unseen dragon. He must have been able to see the creature for when he was furthest from Morty, the man leaped forward, landing on the invisible dragon's back. The creature appeared and twisted and bucked, but the man rode with incredible skill, not to be shaken off.

Then the man plunged the thorn into the dragon's neck, withdrew it, and plunged it in again. With each thrust the dragon bucked and twisted with increasing violence. But the man rode unperturbed. Now green goo dripped from the thorn as the man plunged it in a little lower—perhaps into the dragon's chest—its heart. The dragon became sluggish. Another thrust and the dragon lifted the man high and gave an anguished cry before bringing the man to the ground.

"Oh, you were wonderful," the English lass said, dragging Morty along at the end of the coconut chain as she ran to the man.

The dragon slayer paid no attention to Morty, who bobbed in the breeze several feet above them. "Are you all right, my dear?" he said.

"Who are you?" Morty called down.

The man ignored him. Either he didn't hear or didn't want to.

The dragon slayer said to the woman, "Come, you said you would help that guy find what he seeks—maybe you can do the same for me?"

"You were wonderful," the English lass said to the dragon slayer. "But we shall see about finding what you seek."

Bobbing in the breeze, Morty felt a little relieved—she'd

never tell this guy anything. She didn't have to—he'd already killed the dragon and she was safe now.

The two of them, the man's arm draped over her shoulders, began to walk toward a nearby hill that had just materialized.

But then the man, again without looking up, took the chain of coconuts from the woman. She immediately disappeared. "Where are you taking me?" Morty called down to him.

The man still ignored him.

"Where you taking me?" Morty asked again.

He found out soon enough. The man dragged him like a kite to the thicket and jammed the first coconut tightly between two limbs and walked away. Morty watched the man and his now-you-see-her-now-you-don't date walk hand in hand across the meadow.

The wind suddenly began to blow Morty toward the thorns. An instant later thorns were jabbing at him, sending an electric jolt burning through him. Although he hated the idea, he needed to get back to the thicket. Coconut by coconut, he worked his way down the chain. But when he reached the last one, he recoiled. Inches from it, poised to strike, was the head of another snake, its tongue lapping at the air, its yellow eyes hypnotic slits. Morty back pedaled, moving up the coconut chain. Not to be left behind, the snake slithered forward, one coconut at a time, its evil eyes stalking Morty as they got further away from the thorns.

CHAPTER 9

Morty's heart thundered. The snake moved with deliberate slowness up the coconut chain, its tongue lapping the air, its eyes glued on Morty.

Hoping for some kind of miracle, Morty let the coconuts out one by one, but no miracle came—instead the snake kept coming, its thick body easing onto the vine. Morty looked up. Above was nothing but sky. If he let go he'd drift forever. He made a decision.

He'd had enough for now.

No closer to the formula, he was tired and hurt. Maybe in *real* reality the God he trusted would help him.

Being careful not to let go of the coconut in his right hand, he worked a finger under it and pressed his palm—the escape button.

Virtual reality faded to black, and the suit slowly returned him to what felt like a standing position. "Here I am, back safe," he called out. But instead of a welcoming committee, he was faced with an empty room. "Anybody here?"

"We're in here, Uncle Morty," Kelly's voice called from around the corner. "Something's just coming over the fax from that secret place of yours."

Anxious to see what they'd found, Morty took a couple of steps toward the outer room but stopped. His arms and legs stung from his battle with the thorns. One of his leg wounds hurt even more than the others. He hiked up his pant leg to examine it. It was worse than he thought. About the size of a dime, the electronic shock-induced wound was open and raw and a stream of angry red led from it. There was nothing virtual about this wound—it was real. And it hurt.

But his wounds would have to wait.

Limping slightly, Morty hurried to the computer room and found Tim and Kelly huddled around a fax machine. Mike stood behind them, the kids' excitement having pushed him out of the way.

"Did you find it?" Mike asked Morty, his attention still on the fax.

Morty noticed that the wall clock said 11:30 at night. Everyone seemed to be drooping a little.

"Big thorns—snakes as fat as trees—but no, not the formula." He grinned.

"Wow," Tim said, still not looking up from the incoming fax, "did you get bit?"

"By thorns," he rubbed the painful sore on his calf.

"Oh, no!" Kelly exclaimed. "Are the thorns real in there? They tore right through your pants."

Morty looked down and sure enough, the jolt that had caused his wound had burned through his pant leg. "Electric shock—virtual pain."

Kelly winced at the thought.

Morty said gravely, "There's someone else in there."

Mike's brows dipped inquisitively.

"I suppose he could be part of Matthew's programming, but somehow I doubt it," Morty mused.

"How? There are two suits and one of them's still hanging on the wall."

"Does seem strange, doesn't it?" Morty said thoughtfully.

"Uncle Morty," Tim asked, "this message is addressed to 'Aging Rookie.' That you?"

"In name only," Morty said.

"Here's the first page," Kelly said, handing it to him. Mike read over Morty's shoulder.

"Aging Rookie," Morty read aloud, "we've gone through the data using the block . . ."

"What's 'the block,' Uncle Morty?" Tim asked.

"It should be called 'the city,'" Morty explained. "There's enough supercomputers in the room to fill a city block." He continued reading the curled fax page. "Only one file contains code. We've decoded it—code is sophomoric." Morty eyed the others. "To these guys everything is sophomoric." His head dipped back to the page. "—result on the next couple of pages. I hope we helped. Golden Bits."

"Here's the next page." Kelly grabbed it off the machine just as the third page started grinding out.

Morty's eyes scanned the page silently. Then, "Listen to this," he read, "'I can't believe I'm hearing from him after all these years. I thought he was in jail, but they must have released him . . .'"

"Hammond?" Mike asked.

Morty nodded. "They paroled him after two years," he explained and continued to read: ". . . He's started a company, ChemTech, and, as usual, he's up to no good. He's developed a new bacterium, and he wants me to simulate it and see what it does. There truly is no justice in the world. I've been sweating over recombinant DNA for years, and he goes after it like a hobby and surpasses me. I hate him.'"

"So it did come from Hammond?" Kelly asked, handing Morty the rest of the pages.

Morty read silently. After a moment, Mike said, "Morty, what is it?"

"Oh, sorry—Matthew talks about secretly engaging some of the scientists at Scripps in conversation and picking their brains. Then he goes on here—'The difficult programming seems to be over. The tests were positive. I'll start the simulation tomorrow. Being locked up for nearly a month with this thing is lonely. Thank goodness for Elmer.'"

"Elmer? Who's that?" Tim asked.

"Don't know," Morty shrugged, then continued. "Next entry—these are dated about a year ago. 'The simulation worked well, though I need to make a couple of changes. I should know what this thing is capable of tomorrow. SDSC . . .'" Morty looked up. "The San Diego Supercomputer Center," he quickly explained, "'is giving me some flack about using all eight of their CPUs but to do the simulation in a reasonable time requires them all. Fortunately they owe me a favor.'

"The next entry is two days later. 'Finally finished. His original combination won't work. I've made some critical changes. He's not as smart as he thinks he is. We'll see in a couple days if my changes work and I'm as smart as I think I am.' Then another two days go by, 'When is Cray coming out with the faster machine? I need it. Results are devastating. In a way I wish I'd never listened to Hammond. This thing is horrible. I'm going to run another simulation to check things out.'"

"What did he find?" Mike asked as he saw Morty reading silently ahead.

"Oh, I'm sorry. 'It's as bad as I thought. It'll put people to sleep. It might kill. People over twenty-five seem to be the most vulnerable. I'm not sure what to do. Hammond wants to blackmail countries—even the UN with it. Part of me wouldn't mind being rich. He's formulating a bit of it for real tests. I'm going to keep playing with these simulations. SDSC will let me work during off-hours.'"

"What's next?" Tim asked.

"'I've decided not to think about this for a while. I've turned my attentions back to VR—' he must mean virtual reality," Morty said, "'I've made some incredible progress—object-oriented languages seem perfect for it. I'm able to do a lot very quickly.'"

"Object-oriented languages?" Tim asked.

"Languages that describe objects, their interfaces and interactions with other objects—ADA, the Department of Defense language is like that, C ++ is another."

Tim didn't totally understand, but Morty didn't stop to explain.

"He goes on, 'Because the computer has to be so powerful, Hammond's been able to get me some advanced parts. I don't ask where they come from. Massively parallel systems work well here, though traditional approaches have a place.'" Morty straightened and said, "Here's something interesting. He's given a VR suit to Hammond, and Hammond has a connection into his VR machine remotely. Three T3 links. That's nearly 150 million bits per second. He's got to be close to sustain that kind of speed—a few miles away at most."

"Can we pull the plug on him?" Mike asked.

Morty's brows furled. "No—not a good idea. Unless you know a network intimately you don't want to fool with it. We might mess it all up—ourselves included. I think we'll just have to work around him."

"What's all this mean, Uncle Morty?" Kelly asked.

"It means that Hammond can join me in VR over a very fast telecommunications link." He turned to Mike, "There's no time to go into details, but I think it was Hammond who saved my cookies a couple of times in there—and walked off with my English lass."

Mike sounded concerned. "What kind of danger were you in?"

Morty hiked up his pant leg. The trickle of blood, now dried and grisly brown, still trailed from the wound.

"How'd that happen?" Mike asked, as the kids leaned closer. "Ouch!" Tim groaned.

"A thicket of long, sharp thorns. The suit simulated contact with an electric shock."

"What if they hit your heart?" Mike asked gravely.

"I'm hoping the computer program guards against that. But maybe not—Matthew could have left it up to a random number generator."

"I hope Jesus was in there with you," Kelly said.

Morty smiled. "He's in all reality, Kelly, real and virtual."

"Does Matthew say why he's hidden the formula from Hammond? Does he give any clue where he's hidden it?" Mike asked, stepping over the theological discussion.

"No. He talks more about the VR machine. Ah . . . here's something. 'I'm feeling troubled. Hammond contacted some terrorists today and believes he can get more money over a longer period from them than from blackmail. That means this might actually be used on a broad scale. Can I still draw the line?'"

"Does he?" Tim asked.

"One more entry . . . still about a year ago: 'I spent a long afternoon with Elmer. He and I talked this thing out. He doesn't have much to say on the matter, as you can imagine, but he's with me always. I've an idea about this stuff, and

I'm going to check that out. I'm a brilliant man, and I deserve more than being cooped up in a laboratory all day long . . . people are going to die anyway . . . what's the difference how?'"

Morty put the paper down. "Guess he didn't draw the line."

"But he hid the formula," Mike said.

"In a place where Hammond could find it?" Tim asked.

"Why would he hide it where Hammond could find it?" Morty picked up on Tim's observation. "Hammond's got access to VR. He's smart enough to figure it out."

The outer door pushed open, and Agent Brost stood there, the cat again cradled in his arm. "The hospital just called—Helbert's regained consciousness. They don't think he's . . ."

But Morty and the other three burst past him before he could finish his sentence. They dashed across the street and scrambled through the front door.

Nearly midnight, the halls rang with the echoes of their footsteps as the four headed for the isolation ward.

A young nurse, not used to treating people with much more than measles or mumps, stood scowling at the glass. She pressed down an intercom button. "He's still awake—barely."

"We have to ask him some questions," Morty insisted.

"He may not understand," she cautioned, then, as they rushed to the glass enclosure, she hurried down the corridor to Helbert's room.

A second nurse stood at Matthew's bedside. She held his hand as if comforting a dying man, her eyes cast down in great compassion.

Matthew's lips moved.

"What's he saying?" Mike asked but didn't wait for a reply. "Ask him where he hid the cure to this thing!"

The nurse eyed them irritably, but leaned close to her patient and asked the question. Matthew's lips never stopped moving. The nurse listened for a moment then straightened and shrugged.

"Ask him again!" Mike insisted, and reluctantly the nurse asked Helbert again.

After a moment, Matthew's lips stopped moving and the monitors went back to rest.

The nurse, still holding his hand, laid it gently down and covered it neatly with the powder blue blanket.

"I'm sorry, gentlemen. He was awake, but if he heard me, he didn't respond."

"What was he saying?" Tim asked.

"A prayer."

Morty's brows knit. "A prayer? What kind of prayer?"

"He was asking Jesus for forgiveness. Over and over again. 'Jesus, my Savior, forgive your servant. Jesus, my Savior, forgive your servant.'"

"Is that all?" Mike asked impatiently.

"No," the nurse said, "there was something else."

"What?" More impatience from Mike.

"He said something about Elmer needing milk and a can of food."

"He's a Christian." The thought jabbed Morty like the electric shock from one of those thorns.

"So he got religion. So what?" Mike had been left empty-handed, and he didn't like it.

"*He* came to know Jesus?" Tim, too, sounded amazed.

"How'd that happen?" Kelly asked, also dumbfounded.

"We'll have to wait until he wakes up for the details, but it appears the Lord opened his eyes and did a work in his heart. Maybe the Lord used the guilt Matthew felt as a potential murderer to make him understand he needed a Savior. Only Jesus knows for sure. But this puts a new slant on things." Morty turned to Mike and asked, "Did he have a Bible anywhere in the lab with him?"

Mike shook his head impatiently.

But the nurse said, "He came with it—clutching it. He must have known . . ."

Morty didn't wait. "Can I see it?"

The nurse glanced away as if thinking for a moment. "Oh, yes. We sterilized it, then put it in the refrigerator. We thought he might want it again, and we wanted to kill anything that might be on it. I'll get it for you."

A leather-bound Bible was placed on a tray and pushed

through a slot in the wall. Morty grabbed it and thumbed to the front. "Look, it's dated nearly six months ago, and it's already been beat up pretty bad. The Lord did a real work. Matthew must have felt terrible when he heard what was happening."

"But why didn't he just destroy the formula?" Tim asked. "He said it didn't work without the changes he'd made."

"And if he knew for six months, that's a long time," Kelly said. "Do you still think he was working with his brother?"

"No. I think that's why he hid it," Morty answered.

"I still want to know why he didn't just destroy it," Tim demanded.

Mike fidgeted impatiently and said, "All this is great conversation, but we'd better get back."

Agents Brost and Howard stood quickly when Mike and the others returned. "Did he say anything?" Brost asked, petting the cat's head.

"Something that may be important," Morty said.

"Or not," Mike mumbled.

Kelly tousled the cat's head. "He did say the cat needed milk and a can of food though."

"I thought I saw a small cooler in the computer—wait a minute. What did you say?" Morty asked.

"He said . . . "

Morty stopped her mid-sentence. "Elmer?" He eyed the contentedly purring creature for an instant, then fumbled with the small blue tag on its collar. "Elmer" it read.

"Oh, no!" Morty leaned against the window. "Do you know what this means?"

The two agents eyed one another as Mike stared at them with sharp aggravation. "We're all infected!" Mike groaned.

"What?" Kelly asked, worry woven through her voice.

Tim answered, "That's Helbert's cat. The cat's probably carrying that bug around inside him breathing it all over us."

Kelly grabbed her throat and groaned. Her fear of flight was nothing compared to what she now felt.

Agent Howard slammed Brost in the shoulder with his fist. "I told you to leave that cat alone."

"I like cats," Brost said, defensively.

Morty took charge. "No one comes in or out of here anymore. Call the hospital. We may have infected that whole place. And unless I'm wrong, we're going to get some first-hand knowledge of comas." Then another thought came to life inside his head, and he faced the kids. "You've wanted to help since you got here. Looks like you two are going to get your wish—it's all up to you now!"

"Us?" asked Tim.

Kelly jabbed her brother. "According to Matthew's notes it only hits people over twenty-five, right?" said Kelly.

Uncle Morty looked in their eyes long and hard. "That's right. You're our only hope now—"

Tim gravely eyed his sister, then Uncle Morty. "I guess it's time to pray."

They did.

CHAPTER 10

We need to regroup," Morty said, his face a mask of concern as he stepped into the lab.

"We're gonna die?" Brost clung to the cat, perhaps even tighter now.

"We don't know that," Mike said, "but we do know that if that cat was with Helbert when he was infected, there's a good chance that he's carried the bacterium—or whatever—into the lab."

Agent Howard slammed Brost in the shoulder again, this time harder. "You jerk."

"We've no time for that now," Morty said as he held up a restraining hand. "We need to figure out our next move. You two keep everyone out, and if you feel any symptoms at all, let us know." Morty pushed into the lab and Mike and the kids followed.

Before the door had closed behind them, Mike gestured toward the VR machine and asked, "Do you still think the formula's hidden in there?"

"More than ever," Morty said.

"Why?" Tim asked.

"Because Hammond thinks it is. But he doesn't know where it is either, and he's hoping that I do—or that I know how to find it. That's the only reason he'd save my life in there. He wants me unhurt so I can lead him to the formula."

"But why did Matthew hide it?" Tim asked. "If he's a Christian and the bacterium is as bad as it appears to be, why didn't he just destroy the formula?"

"I don't know, though I have a hunch," Morty admitted. "It doesn't matter, now. What matters is that we've got new information, and we need to figure out how to use it."

Mike sighed. "Other than the fact that we're going to be slipping into nothingness soon, what new information do we have?"

"We know that he's a Christian."

"And?"

"And we know he'll think like one."

"Christians think differently?" Mike challenged.

"Ideally they make selfless decisions, they help their neighbors when things go wrong, they love . . ." Morty explained.

"Selflessly?" Mike splashed the word out with some ridicule.

"Ideally. Sometimes we falter," Morty admitted. "We falter a lot. But this is different. Matthew would have had time to think about things."

"But what difference does it make? It's still hidden in there, and we still have to find it. Quickly—I might add." Mike didn't like the conversation, and it was going nowhere anyway.

Morty said, "What if he wanted just the right people to find the formula? What if instead of hiding it from everyone, he was only trying to hide it from . . ."

Brost's head pushed through the door and gravely told them, "Howard's burnin' up out here."

They found Howard lying on a sofa breathing heavily, beads of sweat popping on his forehead. "It came on suddenly," Brost sounded grim. "I guess the cat is a carrier."

"Keep cold water on him; I think he'll be going under soon," Morty said.

"And . . . I'm not feeling too great either," Brost admitted, looking a little green.

"Well, when you fall, fall into that chair over there," Mike said, sounding overly callous.

"No hospital?" Brost protested.

"All they'd do is monitor you," Morty said. "The best thing we can do is keep going."

"A chair? That's all I get?"

Mike growled impatiently, "Make sure you don't fall and hit your head. We've got work to do."

Morty didn't like Mike's tone, but he couldn't fault his logic. "Take it as easy as you can," he said to Brost, and the four investigators returned to the lab.

"How are you feeling?" Morty asked Mike when they were in the smaller VR room again.

"Not too good," Mike replied, "but then I am a bit of a hypochondriac. Whatever I hear about, I get. Maybe I'm just feeling sympathy pains."

"What hurts?"

"I feel like I'm getting a cold—that general achy feeling."

Morty nodded, "I hate to say it, but me too."

The kids eyed one another. "I guess we'll be able to carry on," Tim said, a hesitant tone in his voice.

"What could you do?" Mike sounded skeptical as well as irritated.

"A bunch," Morty said, "and everything may be up to them."

"You were saying something about how Dr. Helbert might hide the formula?" Kelly asked, trying to get back on track.

"If Matthew wanted to hide the formula from everyone, he could have done that easily. He could have stashed it under some rock in Europe or some temple in Tibet. Who knows? But if he wanted the right people to find it—the people who'd do the right thing with it . . . "

"Then he'd hide it so a Christian would find it," Tim interrupted.

"So they could get on TV and have people donate . . . " Mike mumbled.

"No." Morty ignored the remark. "I believe he discovered something good about the bacterium, as well, something that the world needed. To destroy it would be wrong. But the right people had to find it."

Mike rubbed the back of his neck. He looked pale, and his eyes had developed a crimson rim. "I'm going to lie down. There's an extra chair in the lobby. I guess no matter what your ideas are now I want them to be right." He pushed open the door to the lobby then poked his head back in. "They're asleep out here. I guess I will be soon." His voice was listless and he coughed.

There was no time for sympathy. They had to find the formula soon.

"What are you really saying, Uncle Morty?" Kelly asked.

"I'm saying that you guys are going into VR." Morty looked at each of them in turn with serious eyes. "I think we have to assume that Matthew's going to lead you to the formula somehow. Thinking back to what I saw, he might do it by giving you situations and having you make Christian choices," Morty groaned, teetering slightly. Something had hit him like a high wave and he fell back slightly under the weight of it. He felt his forehead—fever.

"It won't be long for me. I can't believe we're all going at once like this."

"We make Christian choices," Tim repeated.

"Right. And stay together. I've found that virtual reality can hurt. Together you can work the choices out and help each other." Then he remembered something else, "Whatever happens keep going. If you press your palm and escape, when you get back you land in the same circumstances that you left." Morty began working his tongue. "I've never felt so dry. I'd better find a spot to crash. Let's pray—each of us. Me first." As Uncle Morty weakly took Kelly's hand he leaned against the desk. "Lord, please. Please help your servants. Bring what's right to mind when . . ." His head wavered as if he barely had the strength to hold it up.

Tim quickly took over, "Lord in heaven, God of great mercy, give us the wisdom and the courage to succeed."

"And Lord," Kelly added, "if we're going down the wrong path, take us to the right one right away. And be with Uncle Morty. Keep him safe and please, Lord, hurry." She said amen and squeezed Uncle Morty's hand.

Morty slumped against the desk.

The kids caught him, one on either side, and helped him to the floor next to the desk. When he seemed to be sleeping gently, they eyed one another with a mixture of anxiety and calm.

"I guess it's up to us," Kelly said, feeling the sudden weight of responsibility.

"Let's go."

But before they took a step the phone rang in the lobby. Kelly ran to it. "Hello?"

"Who's this?" The voice sounded very official.

"Kelly Craft."

"I want to speak to Agent Brost," the official-sounding voice said.

"He's sleeping."

"Well, I guess you people better know. Maybe you'll work a little harder, maybe you can't work harder. This thing's turned deadly. One of the victims from the lake—a guy named Stark—died about an hour ago."

Kelly glanced at the three men lying in the room and toward the lab where Uncle Morty lay. "Yes, thank you," she said and let the receiver fall gently on the cradle. "Someone's died."

Tim only nodded vacantly and said, "Let's go, Kelly."

Kelly felt all her intense, ago-
nizing fear return as the digi-
tizer door closed in front of her—it was the same fear that
had gripped her when the airplane doors closed, but this fear
was fed by an added element—she was now in total darkness.
But before she could begin beating on the walls, a voice
asked, "Name?"

"Kelly Craft," she answered hesitantly.

"Thank you. Digitizing will begin."

Immediately she was entombed within an electric hum,
and a thin line of light ran down the center of her head, chest
and legs. It was a strange light. Almost an indiscernible blue,
when it made contact with Kelly, it glowed yellow and
ragged, like a million separate threads erupting in fire when
they touched her. The light moved all around her, reading
every contour and when it returned to the front, it faded and
the hum fell silent.

"Thank you, Kelly. Enjoy Helbertland."

The door swung open, and she felt her fear drain away.

Tim, who had already been digitized, stood with his suit
on, but it was still unzipped and his helmet visor was up. He
held her suit out to her. "Scared?"

"I keep saying, 'Trust in the Lord, trust in the Lord.' I think
my truster's broken," Kelly replied.

"Well, you tend to live on the edge of terror, anyway,"
Tim said gently as he helped her into her suit. "We'll be okay.
How tough can it be? It's all make-believe."

Kelly stood on the platform while Tim strapped down her shoes. "Right. Like Uncle Morty's leg wound."

"The one thing we can be thankful for is that no one's gonna see how stupid we look hopping around like bunnies and stuff." Tim laughed as he stepped onto his platform and strapped his own boots down.

"Christian decisions." Kelly breathed deeply to chase the growing panic away.

They eyed each other for one final moment, then the zippers were zipped and the visors came down, securing themselves below the kids' chins.

And the world inside flipped on.

"It *is* just out of *Alice in Wonderland!*" Kelly laughed. "And I can see you."

"Me too."

"You look so lifelike," Kelly exclaimed.

"I am lifelike," Tim laughed, looking around.

They stood in what appeared to be a town square.

"Everything is so real," Tim exclaimed. "Well, not completely real. See how the shadows look too defined?"

Kelly wasn't listening. Her eyes darted from house to charming little house. She was enchanted. The reds, bakery browns, glistening yellows, and deep and powdery blues were vivid, and the houses were brick and gingerbready and not at all like any real houses she'd ever seen.

But the people were what gave it a fairy-tale look. They were, just as Morty had said, chess pieces. Propped atop little legs wearing blue, green, and brown tights and bells tinkling on their fairy shoes, the chess pieces scurried about, babbling to one another.

Tim stood fascinated and at one point laughed when a rook, a horse-shaped fellow with a brilliant golden plume, galloped on his little pair of legs like a child with a broom between its legs.

"I don't think I'm ready for this." Tim laughed.

"I don't want to leave." Kelly also smiled. "But I guess we'd better get going."

"Excuse me, sire," said a pointy-headed bishop with a smiling notch as he nudged Tim.

"Uh, yes?" Tim took a moment to adjust to the fact that he was actually talking to a chess piece.

"Would you like a game, sire?" the bishop asked.

"Not particularly," Tim laughed self-consciously.

"Oh, a shame," the bishop said as he slumped away.

"You've hurt his feelings," Kelly said.

"Uncle Morty said he'd been challenged to a game," Tim said, glancing about. "I guess we have to look for the English lass next."

Kelly scanned the town square, as well. "Tim, there are four ways out of the town square."

Tim nodded, "And?"

"Which one we take will be our first choice and, so far, no one's helped us make it."

"Maybe it doesn't matter."

Kelly shook her head, "I think everything matters in here."

Tim glanced around again. Everything was active—trees rocked, leaves fluttered, and chess pieces bobbed and scampered in all directions. At first they had seemed comical, but they quickly became tiresome. "I'm getting a little tired of all this—let's leave and . . . " But he suddenly stopped.

"Do you see something?" Kelly asked.

"I sure do," Tim said as he stepped toward one of the narrow passages that led from the town square. It lay between a small café and a church. What he saw sat coyly sipping a Coke at a café table.

"Oh, Tim," Kelly moaned.

But even Kelly had to admit, the girl was lovely. Perhaps a little older than Tim, her raven hair and deep almond eyes only added to her soft features. She smiled innocently as Tim approached, her eyes never leaving his.

Tim usually fumbled for words in situations like this, but the girl was too warm, too accepting to trigger any shyness. 'Hi," he said, placing his hands on the iron railing that surrounded the café's patio.

"Hello," she purred.

"My name's Tim."

"I'm Sonya," she said, still just above a whisper.

"Hi, Sonya," Tim cooed.

"For crying out loud, Tim," Kelly said, standing only a few feet away, hands planted disbelievingly on her hips, "The girl's a cartoon!"

"That's my sister," Tim explained.

Sonya's eyes narrowed disapprovingly. "Does she always act like that?"

"Sometimes worse. What brings you here?"

"I enjoy chess," she said, smiling at the pieces that scurried about.

"Tim!" Kelly stood beside him now. "We have to go." She grabbed his arm. But she didn't feel anything. Her hand passed through his image. *That's funny,* she thought.

But Tim didn't notice. His eyes never left Sonya.

"Tim, come on," Kelly injected.

"Keep your shirt on, Kel."

"Uncle Morty's dying, Tim."

Tim immediately straightened. "Right." He looked at Sonya and mumbled, "I have to go. I hope I'll see you again."

Sonya frowned, hurt, but she conjured up a smile and a look that made him feel warm all over—literally. The suit bathed him in warmth. "Good-bye, Fair Prince," she said. "I'll see you soon."

Kelly moved over to a foot-high block of stone. Stepping onto it, she got a commanding view of the square.

Standing on the ground beside her, Tim said, "She was something, wasn't she?"

"She was a drawing. Animation. This whole place is animation. I can't believe it. You're the one with all the logic, and you're standing there getting the hots for a 'toon."

"Well, the 'toon was cute. And I think she liked me."

"Good grief . . ." Kelly grunted. "We have things to do, brother dear." She craned her neck to see the entire square. "But nothing tells us which way to go."

"Excuse me," came a voice and Kelly looked down. A man stood there in tattered clothing, face smudged with grime, eyes sunken and forlorn. His battered hat was clutched upside down in his hand—a beggar.

"We haven't got any money," Kelly said with a touch of

fear, a hard edge to her voice. The man looked so grubby, so disreputable.

"Thank you, anyway," the beggar said and turned to walk away.

"Sir," Tim came alive, "is there anything we can do to help?"

Eyes still glassy, but a bit more alive, the man eyed the two of them. "I ain't eaten in two days."

Kelly, too, began to understand what was happening. She pushed her hand in her pocket and brought out one of several dollar bills she'd brought from home. "Will this help?"

"Will what help?" the old man asked.

Kelly glanced down. Her hand was empty. "I had some dollar bills in there . . . "

"But the digitizer didn't know that," Tim thought out loud.

Suddenly the dollar bill appeared in her grasp. A little surprised, Kelly pushed it again toward the old man. "Will this help?"

"Some," the old man said.

"Would Jesus help?" Tim said, eyes watching the beggar keenly.

"Tell me more." The beggar's expression became expectant.

"When you have Jesus you'll never hunger and thirst again . . . well, that's not actually true. You'll get hungry. I get hungry all the time as a matter of fact. But you'll never be hungry spiritually again. Well, that's not entirely true, either. You'll hunger for righteousness . . . "

"As long at it doesn't have big brown eyes and smile at you," Kelly interjected. "You're doing a masterful job, Tim. May I?"

The beggar's expression became confused. "May I say something?" he asked.

"Sure," Kelly said.

"I wonder if you'd follow me," the beggar said, eying them both expectantly.

Tim smiled at Kelly. "You can criticize me all you want, but don't forget, it was me who got us on the right track."

Kelly nodded appreciatively as they followed the beggar toward one of the lanes out of the square—one that cut between a chess shop and a book store.

Kelly kicked herself for not being more sensitive. How could she have missed an opportunity like that and Tim seen it?

Once they passed the shops the world opened up. The road, rutted by thin wagon wheel tracks, cut a straight path through a wide, green meadow, punctuated now and then by patches of white daisies and gnarled oak trees.

"Where are we going?" Kelly asked the little man who seemed to be picking up speed as his baggy trousers whipped and slapped with increasing insistence around churning legs.

He didn't answer.

"We'll be running soon," Tim said.

Tim's long legs easily matched the beggar's stride, but Kelly's were much shorter and she found the quickening pace difficult. Finally she did have to run.

"Will you slow down?" she gasped. Having worked on the farm all her life she thought herself in good shape, but running after the beggar was curiously hard, like riding one of those exercycles with the tension cranked up. She quickly began to tire.

Kelly remembered that before Morty met the knight in the business suit, the English lass had tired him out.

Were they being worn out? Was there a knight waiting for them somewhere up ahead?

Surely helping and then witnessing to the beggar were Christian things to do? Yet there was no denying the pattern was the same. She and Tim could do nothing but follow—no matter what the pace, no matter what lay ahead.

CHAPTER 12

I can hardly keep up with him," Kelly panted to Tim who galloped beside her, his long gangly legs reaching out much further than hers but for some reason gaining no more ground.

"He's pulling away too," Tim observed, trying to catch up. But it seemed that the harder he ran the further behind he got.

The gingerbread buildings had long since fallen away, and now the rutted path wound through lush country—not unlike home. Clumps of familiar weeds grew on either side, and richly overhanging trees had become more frequent. Had they not been required to run through the place, it might have been pleasant to stop and have a picnic.

"Mister," Kelly called out to the man's back, "can't we stop and rest?"

There was no answer, only an ever-increasing pace and a growing fatigue. Kelly began to breathe in deep, lung-filling gasps. Tim, a member of the school track team, hadn't begun to tire. But the beggar continued to increase his speed, and he finally disappeared over the crest of a hill.

When Kelly and Tim reached the top of the hill, they found the path still there; it led off to an island of bright lights and cheerful music—a carnival. But there was no beggar running ahead of them. He'd vanished.

Kelly stopped, gasping for breath, her heart pounding. "Watch out for the knight."

"The what?"

"The knight. This is when Uncle Morty was attacked by the knight."

"But that's after he hopped around and duck walked."

"That was after they tired him out," Kelly corrected. "And I'm tired out."

Suddenly they heard a loud, rasping snort, and a horse's fearsome whinny, then its breath blew fiery tentacles down their backs. They turned and gasped. They faced the biggest, blackest horse they'd ever seen. Its nostrils flared as it snorted again, its eyes blazing. Atop the massive animal sat Kelly's knight.

A bloodred plume erupted from a steel helmet, the visor down as if for battle. Chain mail draped the knight's shoulders, steel-studded leather gloves held reins in one hand, a two-edged sword in the other. The sword glistened in a darkening sky.

Kelly stood terror-stricken. Tim grabbed at her arm, but his hand melted through her image. He cried out, "Run! We have to run."

Finally, his cries broke through, and she turned and ran—with all she had. She never knew she could run so fast. Legs pounded the ground beneath her, arms flailed at her sides, air crammed her lungs in short, feverish gasps. Beside her Tim ran too. Although he seemed to take two strides for her one, she kept abreast of him. His head was thrown back, his Adam's apple leaping to his chin, his mouth wide as he took in all the air in front of him.

All the time the huge black horse thundered behind them, its hot air pulsing at their backs, the roar of its hooves exploding in their ears. It neither gained on them, nor did it fall away. It was always there, the rush of hot air forever on their necks.

The carnival approached.

Kelly wondered if she'd make it. In the blur of her mind she thought, *This is only a cartoon—a computer-generated graphic.* But then she remembered Morty's wounds, and she immediately wondered what a ton of horse galloping across her back would feel like.

Was there death in virtual reality?

She didn't want to find out. Though muscles ached and lungs screamed, she kept going and Tim kept going and just as she thought she could run no more, the carnival arrived. And as it did, everything ran together in their minds—brilliant red, blue, green, yellow, and pink lights, the joyful music, their pounding hearts, their wretched gasps.

They made it. They ran onto the sawdust field, and abruptly the thunderous hooves fell silent and the hot breath on their necks faded to a cool evening breeze. They staggered to a rail fence and fell against it. Propped there, they allowed their hearts to slow, their screaming lungs to rest, and their muscles to regain strength.

"I've never been so scared in all my life," Kelly finally said.

"You said that when you went to Florida that time," Tim breathed heavily.

"I'm tired. We've been up almost twenty-four hours with time changes. Maybe we ought to get out of these suits and get some sleep."

"What about right here?" Tim suggested.

"Can we sleep in here?"

"Why not?"

Kelly thought about it for a moment. "Sure." She looked around. Not far away were a couple benches. "What about there?"

Tim nodded. "You know, even though we're going to think we're cuddled up on a bench, we'll really be leaning in these suits at a forty-five degree angle."

"Who cares?" Kelly groaned. "Just so I sleep."

A few minutes later, lights glistening off the overhanging leaves, the music chirping in the background, they both drifted off.

▣

Kelly wasn't sure when she first realized she was awake. The music, the lights, the cool evening seemed so much a part of her dream that she drifted into wakefulness as she had drifted into sleep. Rubbing her eyes, she glanced over to Tim's bench, but he was gone. She sat up and looked around.

Still night, the lights danced and blazed, and the music whined.

On her feet, Kelly walked through the sawdust toward the rides and arcade. *Well, where are you, brother?* she mused as she rounded the corner and walked by the ferris wheel, the bumper cars, and one loop-the-loop after another. At each attraction the lines were long, the people laughed and jostled one another, and none of them was Tim.

She rounded the corner to the arcade. The barkers called to her, "Three tosses for a dollar—toss your dime in here and get a goldfish—put the hoop over the milk bottles and win a teddy bear." She had to admit that some sounded like fun, but she had to find Tim. When she reached the end of the arcade she stopped and took a long look around.

The carnival came to Chippewa Falls once a year. Cray Research let them set up in its biggest parking lot, and for three nights the music would play, the rides would bump and spin, and the people would win teddy bears and goldfish. This one looked a lot like that, and for an instant Kelly did what she thought she never would—she missed Chippewa.

"Can I help you, young woman?" the voice came from near her waist. She looked down.

A dwarf stood there, his head a little too large for his egg-shaped body, a friendly smile looking up. She smiled down at him. "Uh . . . I was looking for my brother. Who are you?"

He wore a three-piece suit and wing tips and he bowed deeply. "I'm Harve," he said

"Kelly Craft. Have you seen my brother?"

Harve walked idly back into the arcade, and Kelly walked along with him. "I've not seen your brother," he said. "Have you been here long?"

"No. And you?"

"Years," said the little person. "Are you just passing through?"

"I think so," Kelly said, a bit impatiently. "I really do need to find my brother."

"How did you lose him?"

"We took a nap on one of the benches out front, and when I woke up he was gone."

"Really? Interesting," the dwarf mused, preoccupied with the action at the arcade. "Know the game I enjoy most?"

Kelly frowned. She didn't care. "Which?"

"The squirt gun horse race . . ."

She suddenly remembered the thundering hooves and the stallion's hot breath, "Horses, ugh!" she sputtered, "I really don't want to hear about horses."

"Don't let that earlier episode sour you on horses. They're marvelous animals," Harve stated.

"You know about the . . . "

"Oh, yes," he said with immense understanding. "Not everyone comes in that way, but many do. Sometimes they fall . . . oh, my. Such a ghastly mess." Harve looked up at Kelly. He had a round, loving face with eyes that seemed to search deep inside her. "I've told you an untruth," he said.

"You really don't like squirt gun horse racing?"

He shook his head gravely, "I know where your brother is."

"You do? Where?"

"The show tent . . . talking with that girl."

"How do you know about . . . how'd she get here . . . another horse?" Kelly blurted out the questions.

Harve laughed softly, "She lives here."

"Here?" Kelly glanced around. "In the carnival?"

"We all live here."

"Ah." Kelly understood.

"Your brother's been with her for quite a while now."

"I can imagine," Kelly sighed. "Where are they? We need to get going—although I haven't the slightest idea where."

"May I suggest something?" Harve asked with the deepest gravity.

"Sure."

"I think you should go on alone." Harve's eyes remained on hers.

Kelly's mouth dropped. "You're serious!" she exclaimed. "Alone? Me? I can't do that."

"But he's obviously not serious about your journey."

"He's just a little distracted." Her defense felt uncomfortable. Harve might be right.

"Distracted? It looks more serious than that," Harve replied.

"He's had a rough time lately." Kelly said, looking off toward the show tent. "He's not all that great with girls. He keeps picking the wrong ones."

"But your goal's important."

Kelly cocked her head inquisitively. "You know about our goal?"

"Money is always important."

Kelly shook her head, "It has nothing to do with money."

"Fame, then, or power?" Harve's pudgy legs stepped forward, his moon face pushed closer to hers.

"None of those things," Kelly said flatly.

Harve nodded a huge nod, "Then it truly is important."

"Truly," Kelly echoed.

A stubby finger went up to his chin. "He's not committed. He will let you down."

Kelly took a nervous step away as she said, "Tim's my brother. He won't let me down. Why are you suggesting these things?" *But Tim might be diverted by that girl,* Kelly thought. *This guy might be right.* No. She wouldn't think that way. Tim was a Christian. He might stumble a bit along the way, but he would come through in the end. "Now, where is he? I'll pry him away from what's-her-name so we can get on our way."

"I'll take you there. But first, answer two questions," Harve said, still very serious.

"He's my brother. I won't leave him."

"How important is your journey? Are people's lives at stake?"

"Yes."

"Is one of those lives worth losing over brotherly love?" Harve asked, eyes still large and searching.

Kelly turned her back on the little person and stared across the carnival to the tall, brightly lit tent. A large sign arched over the entrance, rows and rows of red, white, and blue lights spelled "Show." Somewhere in there Tim was ogling Betty Boop.

"Will someone die because . . . "

"Stop it!" Kelly spun around. "He's my brother. I'm going to go get him now. And you're going to stop talking this way. No one's going to die because Tim goes along. Actually, he's smarter than I am sometimes, and I need him to help me find that . . . " She stopped short. She believed Harve didn't know what they were after, and she wasn't going to tell him.

"Okay, but I warned you." Harve's little legs stepped off and he waved her to follow. "Come, little lady."

Kelly followed, still resenting the dwarf's attitude.

The show tent overflowed with babbling, sometimes cheering people. Inside a juggling act spun clubs and chain saws around. But they didn't go in. Harve led her to a small tent off to the side. A dim light glowed from within and cast two shadows on the canvas. It showed two people on a swing that swung lazily to and fro.

Kelly stood in the tent entrance. Neither saw her for a moment. Sonya sat beside Tim, her eyes as large and as seductive as they'd been in town. Tim, on the other hand, had developed big cow eyes. Kelly expected him to moo and paw at the ground any minute.

"Hey!" Kelly blurted.

Tim jumped. "Uh . . . hi, Kelly. I thought you were sleeping."

"I thought you were too." She locked eyes with Sonya, who wore a cotton blouse and faded jeans, like a girl back home might wear, but with a face like that, Tim probably never noticed. "We have something to find," Kelly reminded her brother.

"We were talking," Tim shuffled his feet nervously between glances at Sonya. Her eyes never left his.

"It's time to go."

"You have a wonderful brother," Sonya purred, more to Tim than to Kelly.

"I know. And he needs to get moving. Right, brother?"

He looked back at Sonya, and Kelly saw him melt just a

little bit more. She was relieved when he finally said, "I have to go."

"I have all the faith in the world in you," Sonya placed a warm hand on his arm. "I know you'll do wonderfully."

Tim's heart filled like a balloon, and he seemed to float from the swing. When he reached Kelly he turned back and waved reluctant fingers at Sonya. "I'll see you later," he said.

Kelly just groaned.

When outside, he still looked cow-sad and remained mute until he and Kelly stood beneath the pulsing "Show" sign. Harve had remained in the background, and Tim hadn't seen him yet. Kelly, on the other hand, kept the little man at the corner of her eye.

"I'm sorry I left you," Tim said, sounding repentant.

"I didn't know where you were."

"How'd you find me?"

"That doesn't matter. Tim, we have to keep going. We haven't time . . ."

"I know," he said as if resigned to the fact.

"Of course, I don't know where we're going next. Maybe we ought to pray about it."

"A virtual prayer?" Tim said, with a small laugh.

"There's been no decision for us to make . . ."

"Miss and Mr. Craft, may I speak?" A small voice came from behind.

"Who's he?" Tim asked.

"Harve," Kelly answered.

"Harve who?"

The dwarf stepped forward, "Just Harve. I have a door to show you."

"A door?" Tim repeated.

"Where?" Kelly asked. "Where does it go?"

Harve was close to them now, and he looked up and smiled broadly. "Come," he said, "your search continues."

CHAPTER 13

"Y ou said something about a door. What door?" Tim asked impatiently. They'd followed the little man in the three-piece suit for what seemed like forever. Now the blazing lights of the carnival were only a memory, and a flat-faced moon lit the country path they walked along.

"It's up ahead here," Harve called back to them, his short legs moving quickly.

"Did you get enough sleep?" Kelly asked Tim.

"Some. I drifted off fast enough, but then I woke up and decided to look around."

Kelly sensed a strain between them. Tim never liked her mothering him, and dragging him away from Sonya fell into that category—no matter how good the reason.

"I had a dream," Kelly said idly.

"And?"

"I don't remember it. It just seems funny having dreams while wandering around virtual reality—like a dream in a dream. I begin to wonder what's real. Do you think Jesus is in here too?"

"He's everywhere," Tim answered mechanically.

"I guess. Think about this one. We're in this world being created by electrons that do millions, maybe billions of instructions per second, and Jesus can interrupt them at just the right instant. He'd have to do that in here. Wouldn't he?"

"I guess," Tim said.

"Are you going to be mad at me forever?" Kelly finally asked.

"I'm not mad," Tim insisted.

"You are and you know it."

Tim didn't answer. Actually there was no time to answer. They had come to the door.

In the ghostly glow of moonlight, they nearly bumped into it. The wooden door cut a narrow archway through a long wall that stretched endlessly in all directions—right, left, and up. Without hesitating, Tim grabbed the brass handle, but it only jiggled.

"Patience," Harve admonished.

"What's inside?" Kelly asked the dwarf, her eyes narrowing with interest.

"We're inside. That's outside," Harve pointed out.

"Great. We've come this far for an English lesson," Tim sighed.

"It's called semantics, the study of meanings," Harve corrected. "And it's an important distinction. Inside is safe, outside isn't," Harve said smirking at Tim.

"It's not safe?" Kelly's heart grabbed mid-thump.

"Let's just hope Jesus has his instruction counter working," Tim said with a faint note of sarcasm.

"Son . . ." Harve began, but then interrupted himself as if deciding that his words be lost on the boy. After a quick, frustrated wave of his hand, he turned to Kelly. "I'll be opening the door now. There will be no turning back once you're outside. Jesus will be with you," with a glance at Tim, he continued, "and with you."

"You're a Christian?" Kelly asked the dwarf.

"A product of my Creator." Harve bowed again. "Now, here goes." The little man grabbed the handle, levered it down, and the door swung upon.

Beyond the door was blackness.

Kelly stepped cautiously toward the arch while Tim, though hesitant at first, quickly overcame his reserve and stepped past Kelly and through the doorway. "I can't see anything," he called back to Harve.

"You won't until the door is closed," Harve stated.

"You mean we won't know what's outside until there's no way back?" Tim frowned.

"Does that make a difference?" Harve asked. "Is your mission one that would allow you to stop here?"

"No, it isn't," Kelly said and realized that they had no choice. She stepped through the door.

"Are you two ready?" Harve asked.

"As we'll ever be," Tim said.

"Close it." Kelly cringed.

The door closed.

Instantly daylight appeared. With the door behind them, they faced a never-ending shadow, with a thicket hovering over it.

"Oh, wow!" Tim said, words crammed with awe.

"Look at those thorns!"

"Uncle Morty mentioned thorns. I wonder if this is where he was."

"Snakes too," Kelly remembered Uncle Morty's tale. "I'm not sure I want to go under there."

"I'm not sure there's any other choice." Tim took a deep breath and said, "Come on."

Kelly hesitated, but Tim's first step pulled her along. Being with him was far better than being left alone, snakes or no snakes.

Wait! Kelly's heart suddenly began to flutter. *What's happening?* "Tim . . . ooooooooo!"

"I'm floating," Tim exclaimed.

Their feet left the ground, and both rose toward the thorns. Arms flailing about at first, they quickly realized that panic didn't help. Forcing a calm, they each grabbed for a lower limb and though each suffered a minor thorn prick, after a moment or two they bobbed out of immediate danger.

"So this is what helium balloons feel like," Kelly muttered.

"Uncle Morty must have made it through here. How'd he do it?"

"I hear something," Kelly said anxiously, her eyes darting to a thousand places, her ears straining. Then she relaxed. "I guess it's just the wind knocking these things together."

Tim, on the other hand, carefully studied the area around him. The solution had to be hidden somewhere in all these thorns and vines.

"Dad would know what to do," Kelly lamented.

Tim stopped.

"What do you see?" Kelly's panic returned.

"You're right. Dad told us what to do."

"Huh?"

"He said to take advantage of our talents."

"And?"

"And right now our talent is floating. We could float on top of all this stuff."

"On top?"

Tim didn't try to explain. Hand over hand he worked his way along the bottom of the thicket back toward the wall.

Kelly, not as agile as her gangly brother, found herself at war with some of the smaller thorns, but before long, she, too, had made it to the edge of the thicket.

"Now we work our way up the side," Tim directed. "Since we float, that ought to be easy enough."

Kelly peered into an endless sky, "But what if we don't hold on?" Her heart fluttered uncontrollably now. Being up in the clouds in a plane was bad enough, floating around up there waiting to fall would be unbearable.

"Don't think about it."

"I can't help it."

"Push your palm if that happens."

"And what good will that do?" Kelly groaned. "When I come back I'll still be floating off into eternity."

"Then I'll have to go on alone."

"Without me?" Kelly said, sounding hurt.

"I guess," Tim said. He didn't like the idea either. "Just hold on, and we won't have to worry about it, will we?"

"No. I guess not." Kelly felt a pout of resolve come on. There was no time to waste worrying—there was only time to get it done.

"Here goes." Tim grabbed a branch on the edge of the thicket and floated to the next branch, which was a vine.

Before Tim knew it, the vine unwound from somewhere within the thicket and he floated up and out. "Grab the vine!" he cried. But before she could, the vine stopped short and Tim floated and bobbed in the wind like a kite. "Hey, this is neat."

"You're nuts," she called up, unable to imagine how floating above a sea of thorns could ever be neat.

"I can see forever up here," he called down. "There's a hill off on the horizon."

"Really?" Kelly moaned. "How wonderful." She grabbed another limb, and this time she drifted into a thorn. It dug into her side, and the point's electric shock sent a shrill pain through her.

"You okay?"

"No, I'm not," she fired back, working up the courage to grab another branch and float up another foot or two. Only a couple more feet and she'd be above the thicket.

"Keep at it," Tim encouraged, still floating. "There's a castle or something on the top of the hill. Maybe we're supposed to go there."

"Maybe," Kelly answered distractedly.

"I guess I'd better come down," Tim said and began to work his way, hand over hand, down the vine. When he was even with the top of the thicket, he grabbed a thorn that extended a little further than the others and pulled himself in.

About that time Kelly, too, reached the top.

"It's like a bed of nails," Kelly said as she surveyed the endless mat of tangled thorns and branches.

"We'll just walk on our hands," Tim said cheerfully. "Our feet will float, and we should be at the end of this thing in no time."

"It goes forever," Kelly sighed.

"It can't. Dr. Helbert will have something else in mind for us soon." Tim looked off into the distance, then added, "I hope so, at any rate." He grabbed the first branch then the second. "Come on, you're the impatient one."

Kelly let that remark pass and felt her legs rise in back of her as she grabbed the closest branch with her right hand, then grabbed the next with her left. "You're right. It's not that hard. At least we're not getting stabbed."

Tim "walked" along beside her. "I need to apologize to you," he said after a few minutes.

"No you don't," Kelly said, letting him down lightly.

"I lost my head back there."

"She is beautiful. And Dr. Helbert programmed her to steal your heart."

Tim sighed. "I know."

They moved quickly. Once Kelly grabbed a vine by mistake and drifted out a few yards before it stopped abruptly. The sensation brought both panic and exhilaration as her screams melted to nervous laughter. It was almost fun.

And that's when the snake sprang up before Kelly—its mouth gaping, tongue flicking, eyes a savage yellow.

Her scream flooded her throat, then broke from her mouth, her eyes closed with the force of it. When they opened again, they filled with bloodred terror. She stared directly into the serpent's mouth.

Immobilized for but an instant, Tim recovered and grabbed for a branch to propel him toward Kelly. "Hang on, I'm coming," he yelled.

But the snake had no intention of waiting for Tim's arrival. It coiled back in preparation to strike.

Kelly hung on petrified. At any moment those sharp teeth would close around her throat and she'd have no defense.

Tim pushed himself toward her. Although only a few yards away, he found that the thorns between them presented a jagged barrier. But with Kelly in trouble he couldn't think about that now. He grabbed another limb, then another, his arms stinging as they scraped the thorns' dagger-like points.

Kelly's heart refused to beat as the snake's head coiled back.

It sprang. Mouth gaping, teeth bared, tongue flicking, it came right for her eyes.

Kelly pushed back and in doing so lost hold of her limb. She grabbed for it, but it was already out of reach. She flailed as if trying to swim back, but her fierce attempts only drove her further away.

The snake's head stopped just short of her face. An ugly smile drifted from ear hole to ear hole. "Boo!" it said.

Kelly heard the sound as the wind caught her, and she began to drift higher and higher into the sky.

"I'm sorry, Tim. I'm so sorry," she called out.

Tim's face turned up to her. "Kelly! I'll see you soon," he cried. Although his words faded as the distance between them grew, she heard sorrow in them. She also saw the snake's triangular head turn its attention to Tim.

CHAPTER 14

As Tim saw Kelly drift further and further away, he lost track of the snake. But only for a blink of an eye. For out of the corner of his eye he suddenly saw the snake approaching. It had already pulled several feet of its thick, muscular body from the thicket and moved toward him like determined ooze.

"Hello," the snake hissed, "welcome to my home."

"Some welcome," Tim spat, looking desperately for an escape. Humanity's hope rested squarely on him, and he knew he couldn't afford to just drift away as Kelly had.

"Actually, that is exactly how I welcome intruders. I hate people, you see. I roam here and there seeking people to devour," said the snake with a touch of elegance.

"Well, you won't devour me," Tim insisted. However, his boast seemed quite hollow at the moment. He moved back a "step," eyes scanning the thicket for a weapon.

"Your hands seem quite juicy," the snake said, easily closing the gap between them. As he slithered closer malicious yellow eyes locked on Tim's hands.

"You're just a computer graphic," Tim heard himself say, and he felt renewed courage.

"Oh?" replied the snake. "Does a graphic feel like this?" It lashed out at Tim's left hand.

The moment the mouth closed around it, pain shot up Tim's arm, his hand ravaged by tiny pricks that seemed to sink deeply into his tissues. When the snake drew its teeth away the pain persisted.

The snake smiled. "Shall I try the other one?"

"No!" Tim fired back, yet to prevent the next attack he would have to let go and drift away—and that would mean people could die.

His eyes darted around as he "stepped" quickly back again. This time he grabbed a thorn with his good right hand; to his surprise, it broke off. Holding it, he quickly grabbed another with his injured left hand. This one held fast. He looked up. The snake eyed the thorn in his right hand with concern.

Tim couldn't believe how dumb he'd been. He was surrounded by weapons and now he held one.

Tim brought the thorn up like a sword and waved it in the snake's face. "Now it's your turn."

The snake drifted back, then snapped forward. It took the thorn in its teeth, tore it from Tim's hand, spit it out, and smiled triumphantly.

Tim grabbed another thorn. This one remained firmly attached to its branch. He grabbed another, then another. Neither gave way.

"Frustrating, isn't it?" the snake hissed a laugh. "I've lived here all my life. I love the thorns. And they love me."

Tim grabbed a fourth.

"Now," said the snake, "prepare for your hand to leave your arm."

At that moment, the hand that was the snake's target grabbed a thorn that came loose with a snap. As the snake's head moved forward, Tim brought the thorn up. It caught the snake just below the jaw and went on to break through the top of its head. Tim let the thorn go as the snake, caught in the anguish of its pain and its war against its own death, whipped about on the top of the thicket. In doing so it stabbed itself repeatedly on other thorns, and after throwing blood everywhere, it finally fell among its beloved thorns, dead.

Tim's heart still thundered, his lungs still pumped, as he took a moment to calm down. He'd never faced anything like this before and for a moment the fear of losing swept over him. But he hadn't lost—he'd won. "Thanks, Lord," he said, and then wondered if he ought to be really thanking Helbert. No, he'd thanked the right one.

His legs still floating behind him, Tim took up his "walk" again.

Floating weightlessly, Kelly saw the thicket drift further and further away. Although she tried to keep Tim in sight, after only a few minutes that became impossible. Defeated and frightened, she prepared to escape to reality by pushing her palm, when she felt a surge of air pick her up and carry her.

She'd hit a jet stream, a current of rushing wind, and it was supporting her. She glanced down. The world was a blur thousands of feet below. What if the stream ended? What if she drifted out of it? What if she suddenly began to weigh something again?

Her concerns bounced like Ping-Pong balls in her head until the panic she'd felt when she let go returned. Her muscles tightened, her heart fluttered, and she felt a scream coming on.

But the stream held, and she didn't gain weight. Before long she began to relax again. These times of relaxation, however, were each short-lived. Every time she hit an air bump, or the stream dropped her slightly, her muscles tightened again and her heart leaped to her throat.

She also quickly realized that she didn't have to tumble uncontrollably. If she put her arms out and threw her legs back, she stabilized and for a while she felt a bit like Superman.

The castle Tim had seen approached quickly, and the closer it got, the blacker and more sinister it became. Its spires reached up like daggers; its dreary walls peered at the world through arched windows with flickering yellow lights—which were reminiscent of the snake's eyes. Kelly thought for a moment that she'd fly straight into it, but the wind current picked her up and as she flew over, she saw a web of walkways leading to and from the dark, forlorn buildings.

She saw no life except the yellow glow from the castle's many windows.

Once past it, though, she saw nothing. A desert plain stretched before her as far as she could see. If Helbert wanted her to be a part of the search again, he'd picked a strange place to take her.

Tim saw two other snakes as he "walked" along. They left him alone, but they didn't run away from him. They were each wound within the thicket and hard to pick out, but when he did, they were unmistakable. Decorated in shadowy patterns, they were hard to see until the sun hit them, then their skin glowed orange and seemed flecked with red. They were ominously beautiful. Tim had to smile. Maybe some of Uncle Morty's artistic leanings were rubbing off on him—though Tim knew he'd never paint a barn blue with clouds and lightning.

He suddenly wondered how Uncle Morty was. He wondered if he should take a moment and see what was happening outside the suit. And then, in the back of his mind, he heard a phone ring and someone on the other end telling him that someone else had died. No, there was no time. Wherever this thicket went, he'd have to follow it.

Another snake lay resting along a branch deep within the thicket. Tim "walked" right above it, his hands causing a shiver in the thicket. The snake moved and Tim stopped.

He seemed to be getting near the end of his "walk." The land beyond took on shape and color. The last thing he wanted was to let this snake get between him and whatever would happen next.

He grabbed at a thorn nearby. To his surprise it gave way, and he tore it off. Placing it between his teeth, he kept walking. The snake lay still again. Maybe it would leave him alone, as the others had.

Step by step Tim worked his way up the snake's body. It seemed to never end, but finally he came to the head. It lay in the fork of a branch as if sleeping. Tim's eyes riveted on the head, fully prepared to drive the thorn through it if it moved. But it didn't, and he made his way past.

The thicket came to an end.

Only a few yards later Tim took hold of a branch, pulled himself forward as he had a thousand times before, and found himself staring over the edge, about twenty feet above a brown meadow.

"What now?" Tim said to whomever might be listening.

Suddenly pain fired up his arm. His hand seemed engulfed in a million pinpricks that sank deep between the bones. He screamed and saw the snake's head gnawing it.

He grabbed for the thorn in his teeth and was about to stab at the head, when it let go and the bloodred mouth opened to attack his face. Tim jabbed with the thorn, but the snake deftly grabbed it away and spat it to the ground below.

Before it could turn back, Tim leaped out of the way. His ravaged hand still burning, he disregarded the pain as best he could and grabbed another thorn, but this one held fast. Then for another, but the limb gave way. It was a vine, and it uncoiled and let him float about ten feet above the thicket before it caught.

Relieved for just an instant, Tim grabbed the vine with his other hand in an attempt to give his injured one a rest. The searing pain subsided slightly.

"What you doin' up there?"

It was a woman's voice. He looked down. He could see no one, yet it came from just below him.

"I can't see you."

"You can't until you touch me. Want to touch me?" she said.

Before Tim could answer, the snake came to the base of the vine. Its black tongue flicked at him several times, and then the massive head peered up the vine at him, yellow eyes filled with images of Tim's destruction.

"I'd like to touch you more than anything else in the world at this moment." Tim said to the person he couldn't see. "Can you help me?"

"No, not really," the voice said, revealing distress. "Actually, I need some help of my own."

"I guess that makes two of us." Tim spoke with a voice bound by panic. The snake's head began to inch forward.

Now the voice sounded near tears. "Do you know how to stop a dragon?"

The snake's body was now on the vine, its tongue testing the air.

"Stop a dragon?" Tim asked. "I really can't talk to you now."

"But I need your help!" she called up, agitated.

Tim's hand still ached, and a shaft of pain fired up his arm. He groaned, wanting to grab his arm and massage it, but he couldn't let go of the vine. The snake inched closer.

The voice repeated, "Please, I really do need your help."

"I can't help." Tim couldn't believe he was even being asked. "I can't even see you."

"Please, help me. Please."

Tim bobbed at the end of the ragged vine, the tremor of the snake's incessant movement vibrating in his hand. The reptile was a foot closer, its tongue hissing.

How can I possibly help? How? Tim thought, wondering why she was even asking. The snake was gaining speed, and every moment Tim took to consider the approaching dragon was a moment away from finding the solution to his own problem. Yet a strong part of him wanted to help.

"I have a riddle," the woman's voice broke through anxious tears. "You have to help me answer the riddle. In a minute that horrible green monster's going to come around that hill over there, and if I don't have an answer to his riddle he's going to tear me apart."

The serpent's head climbed another six inches. Tim's good hand would soon be in range. "Talk fast," Tim urged. His ten-foot vine now had five feet of snake on it.

"It goes like this: 'Out of the eater, something to eat; out of the strong, something sweet.'"

"That's it?" Tim asked incredulously.

"Can you help?"

It didn't seem like a riddle, and yet it sounded familiar. Why? Where had he heard it before?"

"Please. Think hard. I can hear it coming."

To Tim's surprise, he could hear it coming too—raspy breathing, thunderous footsteps.

"I've heard it somewhere before," Tim called down.

"Please think. My life is at stake."

The snake crept closer.

"Where? Where?" Tim searched his memory. "Out of the eater . . . " he muttered as if the sound would bring it to mind.

"It's getting closer!" The thunderous footfalls drummed louder, the raspy breathing grew more intense.

And then, as if a light went on, he knew. He cried out, "It's Samson's riddle—Judges, the book in the Bible—it's the lion that Samson killed that bees made a hive in. The eater's the lion, the honey's sweet."

"Oh, thank you so much—thank you," the voice called back in immense triumph.

But there was no triumph at Tim's end of the vine. The snake slithered within a yard of him now.

"Can you be some help to me now?" Tim called down to the invisible woman.

"Me? How?" the voice returned.

"Can you tear off a thorn and toss it up to me?"

"Me? Tear off a thorn?" The voice sounded mystified. "I'm sorry. I don't do things like that."

"But I just . . ."

The snake suddenly lifted its head. It had heard Tim's plea refused, and now it laughed, an evil, breathy laugh.

Below, the invisible dragon crashed to a halt in front of the invisible woman as she cried out the answer to the riddle. After a huge roar of disappointment from the dragon the snake laughed again.

"You think you have me, don't you?" Tim called down to the snake.

The snake smiled and nodded vigorously. It opened its mouth and with a quick snap, cut the vine.

"Oh, no." Tim cried out. Still holding the severed end, Tim watched as snake, thicket, invisible woman, and invisible dragon dropped away from him.

Tim's heart sank to the pit of his burning stomach. He'd let everyone down.

CHAPTER 15

Cradled in the rushing wind, soaring with miraculous freedom, at times resting, as if in the hand of God, Kelly swept along high above an infinite table of land. The castle had long since disappeared over a now distant horizon, and nothing could be seen in any direction. At first she'd wondered what would happen next, then she relaxed once and for all and enjoyed the rich sensation of flight. She found herself laughing as the thrill became inexpressible any other way. Was this how Peter Pan felt, or Superman, as they flew over a spinning world below?

Soon, however, the thrill gave way to impatience; she wondered again what would come next.

She even prayed about it.

As she prayed she wondered if the Lord would change the instructions the computer was grinding out to answer her prayer. But when her prayer died away to a wistful amen, nothing changed.

Until suddenly the rush of wind stopped, and the hand that held her dumped her out.

She screamed once, and then her screams caught in her throat, as she fell faster and faster toward the hard earth. She took a breath, but her lungs wouldn't fill. She tried to scream, but no sound emerged. She tried to look down, but her head wouldn't move. She tried to stick her arms out in a vain effort to arrest her descent, but her arms were plastered to her side.

She fell like a rock. What would hitting the earth at a million miles per hour feel like?

Mustering all her strength, she forced her head down and

saw a bit of ground rushing up. Still brown, still a desert, a new feature presented itself as a possible splattering site—a canyon.

She couldn't watch, and yet she couldn't keep from watching. "Oh, Lord—show a little mercy here," she prayed through lips pressured back by the roaring air.

A large black crow appeared. It flew by, did a double take, and glided over to her. Although the air blasted by her, the bird glided effortlessly on a cushion of it. It eyed her squarely and then glanced toward the ground. After shaking its head and tsk-tsking at her, it soared away.

A second later she hit. Water.

Cold, churning, angry water. Dirty brown water with white billows springing up and swirling about.

She went under then bobbed to the surface. She spun, tumbled, bounced off boulders like a pinball, and fought for breath. She'd landed in the canyon, and the canyon convulsed with rapids.

Hey, Lord! she tried to scream, but her lungs couldn't find the air to do it.

She was tossed to the surface again and finding a spot where the world seemed just a bit less traumatic, she tried to look around. The canyon walls rose sheer and rusty brown on either side. About fifty feet across, the river was full of boulders that were painted that same rusty brown, boulders of all shapes and sizes, boulders around which the water pitched and swirled, boulders that made locating the shore impossible. The river pulled at Kelly, forced her under, expelled her up, and dragged her further down the rapids.

Then the currents quickened. For an instant, she seemed to be on a water slide, and the sensation brought a cheer to her lips as she slid into a deeper, calmer pool. Seizing the opportunity, she swam for a ribbon of sand that appeared on the edge. But an underwater current grabbed her and washed her further downstream.

More rapids. More boulders. More currents. More white fists of water battering her. Yet for all the jostling and growing number of bruises, Kelly felt supremely safe. She was on the ground—a liquid ground—but the ground nonetheless.

She came to another deeper, calmer pool and another beach that spread out peacefully in the sun. Feeling the gravel give way beneath her feet, she struggled to the sand. Exhausted, she bathed herself in the warm sunshine. Minutes passed. A big part of her wanted to lie there and just let the world go by for a long while. But then a bigger, more insistent part reminded her of the race she ran—against death.

Over the incessant roar of the water Kelly heard another sound—a chilling, ghostly wail. The noise came from the canyon wall and pulsed and faded to an eerie moan that floated on her nerve endings. She turned her head toward it. Not far away stood a huge boulder. Shaped like a gigantic spearhead, it broke through the sand a few yards from the canyon wall. The unearthly howl came from behind it.

"Well, Lord, what now?"

She looked around. The river, though a pool now, fell away a little further down, and Kelly suspected that there were more rapids ahead. The canyon wall dropped from the sky and presented an unscalable, impenetrable barrier. On the other side of the pool, the wall fell to the water in the same way, except there was no beach. If a computer-generated monster lived behind that rock, there were few opportunities to escape it. Kelly could brave the rapids, but her arms and legs still ached from the last assault.

She struggled to her feet.

The wail had died away slightly. However, after Kelly took a couple of steps, it reasserted itself. Clothing wet, skin chilled from a growing breeze, she moved with an uncharacteristic boldness toward the spear-shaped boulder. But when she reached it, caution returned. The howl changed. Although still an animal's cry, it wailed in such torment that horrific shivers danced up her spine. Had the sound hands it would have clutched her soul with icy fingers.

She eased around the boulder, muscles stiff, prepared to confront something even more hideous than the thicket snake.

"Harve!"

The dwarf, still in his three-piece suit, knelt in the sand behind the rock. His pudgy hands cupped over his mouth, he wailed with uncompromising fury—until he heard his name. Then he stopped and looked up with a sheepish grin.

"What are you doing?" Kelly asked as fright dissolved to laughter.

"Howling."

"But why?"

"I'm not sure really. I just had the urge," he said as he glanced about himself and grunted. "A second ago I was at the carnival. Now I'm here. There's something very unstable about my line of work."

"What line of work is that?" Kelly asked, still feeling relieved to see a familiar face.

"Computers. I'm in computers," Harve said gravely. "Well, what now?"

"What do you mean,'What now?' I'm supposed to ask you that. I've just fallen out of the sky into a raging rapids and been cast ashore on this beach. Your howling brought me over to investigate."

"Maybe it had something to do with this cave," Harve said, turning his back to the boulder and facing a large, black, airless opening in the canyon wall.

Kelly couldn't understand how she'd missed something so large. It was definitely a cave. She took a step inside, and when her eyes grew accustomed to the dark, the passage grew deep with irregular shadows.

"Do we go inside?" Kelly asked as she turned.

But Harve wasn't where he'd been.

She stepped from the cave. Her eyes squinted in the light as she ran to the other side of the boulder. The beach was empty. Harve was gone.

A strong sense of being alone swept over her. She ran around the boulder again, but still no Harve. Then she looked at the black hole in the canyon wall. "Are you in there somewhere, Harve?" she muttered. "Did you wake up in there now? Are you waiting for me?"

She bit her lower lip, swallowed her fear of the unknown, and stepped inside.

The floor lay coated in a thick carpet of sand and cut a narrow passage through the stone. Although the light from the opening faded quickly behind her, light from a different source cast the cave in unearthly shadows. One step followed another and soon Kelly was on her way.

Time faded as the cave twisted and turned through the rock. Now and then the floor climbed but then it would descend. When it cut right, it would soon cut left. Kelly had the distinct impression she was walking further and further from the river and at nearly the same level.

It all seemed very boring and, like her ride on the winds, there seemed little purpose to it all.

Then the cave split—a fork. One cavern went left, the other right. Which way should she go?

She thought back to everything she'd experienced in Helbertland. She thought back to all her dad's advice. She thought back to every Scripture verse she could remember. She thought back to every book she'd ever read, every conversation she'd ever had.

None of it told her whether to go right or left. If she had had a coin she would have flipped it.

She hated these kinds of decisions. Last winter, the youth group put her in charge of deciding whether they should go to a hockey or a football game. She stewed about the choice for three days. She chose the football game, and only after they arrived did she remember the weather forecast. It snowed fourteen inches in three hours. The youth group never asked her to plan an outing again.

After standing at the fork for several minutes, Kelly chose left, and immediately wondered what she was forgetting. What made the choice even more suspect occurred a few steps later. From somewhere at the end of the tunnel, swallowed by tons of rock, came a howl—that same, horrific howl.

CHAPTER 16

As the world fell away, the three-foot length of vine still clutched in his hand, Tim felt an overwhelming sense of defeat. He'd let down the whole world! It hadn't been his fault. But it didn't matter. If he'd only thought ahead, or done something differently . . .

Now all he wanted to do was drift forever. Maybe after a while they'd just bury him—unplug him from the wall and just bury him, black suit and all.

The Lord's in control.

The thought came at him like an arrow. But it didn't stick. Rather, another current of defeat pushed it off course, and the arrow disappeared somewhere in the back of his mind.

A rush of air blasted by. As if Tim were a leaf on an autumn day, it scooped him up. At first conflicting currents spun and tumbled him about, but after a few anxious moments he'd worked himself into a stabilized position.

He was being carried along.

The tide of defeat weakened, and a renewed sense of purpose and hope replaced it. The castle, bright and sparkling in the crisp sunlight, waited for him ahead.

"Thanks, God," Tim said.

As he approached the castle, he got a better look at it. The gray stone walls seemed to grow from the surrounding crags and several spiked spires poked at the sky. Although there was a sinister aura about the place, it was almost covered by the pageantry. Red and blue flags flew from every parapet, and flapped majestically in the breeze. A crowd roared excitedly somewhere below.

And Tim flew by . . .

By?!

He couldn't just fly by! Stretching arms out like wings, he maneuvered toward one of the spires. Then, when the moment was right, he grabbed for it. Like a ring spinning around a post, his arms locked around the top, and he spun gracefully down. He came to rest gently on the stone railing bordering a stone stairway that wound down the side of the stone spire.

From his perch Tim could see the roaring crowd and the object of the roars—a medieval joust. Stacked in two opposing stands, two crowds cheered wildly as two knights on horseback, one garbed in red, the other in blue, exploded toward one another, lances leveled.

A moment later, as one side erupted in cheers, the other side in jeers, the blue knight buried his lance squarely in the red knight's chest. The crimson warrior was suspended by the impact for a split second, then fell like a sandbag to the ground. The crowd "whooshed," as the armor slammed the dirt.

A Cadillac ambulance, its red light flashing, siren whining, sped from a tent on the far end of the arena. Three men in white outfits scooped the fallen knight up, tossed him on a gurney, shoved him in the back, and drove back to the tent.

Tim's brows furled. There was something definitely wrong with that picture.

"'Scuse me." An English accent popped up at him.

Tim looked down. An old man with a neatly cropped gray beard, wrinkled eyes, and a page's brown leather uniform stood in front of him. He held a long stick and tapped Tim's leg with it.

"M' name's Barney and you'll be needin' this," the old page said.

"I will?" Tim grabbed the stick and eyed it with suspicion. "What is it?"

"Magic wand," Barney said.

"Magic wand?"

"Do I stutter? 'At's wha' I said. Magic wand."

"What do I do with it?"

"Magic. Wha' else? Turn people to toads. Things like that."

"Why would I want to do that?"

"Why not? Better'n walkin' about in a silly leather costume like 'iss handin' out things to idiots."

Tim had to admit that was probably true. "Where am I, anyway?"

"The Castle."

"Which castle?"

"This one. Listen, I'd love to stand 'ere and chat wi' ya for hours—it's so stimulatin' an' all—but I got other fish to fry."

"Really. What other things are you doing?"

"Fryin' fish. For the tournament." Barney pointed, then said, "You really do need 'iss 'ere wand. If you can manage these stairs it'll be magic." The little man turned to leave.

"Wait. What am I supposed to do here?"

"Don't know. Don't really care much."

Tim eyed the stick suspiciously and asked, "How does this work?"

"Like all magic wands, for cryin' out loud." Barney said, waving a frustrated hand at Tim before disappearing down the stairs.

Tim eased off the railing onto the stairs and stared at the wand. It was a tree limb. The bark had been peeled off and the stick sanded smooth, but there were still telltale bends and twists.

Was he to say magic words? "Abracadabra," he muttered. Nothing. Then he pointed it at a flag nearby and said, "Abracadabra." Still nothing. "Stupid thing."

The flagpole exploded, and the red flag, waving idly, toppled to the stairs below.

"That's interesting." Tim's eyes grew very large.

He pointed it at another flag. "Stupid creep!" he shouted. This time the explosion was even greater. That flagpole, now in flames, fell and clattered below.

"Hmmmm." Tim got the picture now.

A spire poked at the clouds about fifty feet across a

cobbled square. A large flag waved above it, the flagpole held by a statue—a cherub with fat arms and fat legs and a round tummy with a deep little belly button. The belly button became Tim's bull's-eye.

Resting the wand across a raised arm he sighted down it. This was a little more tricky. With the slight bends and twists he wasn't exactly sure where the thing was pointing, but . . .

He summoned up a lungful of air, tightened his chest and diaphragm, and cried, "Nerd!"

A truer shot Davy Crockett never made. The stone belly button exploded, the fat arms burst at the shoulders and flew off, the wooden flagpole ignited and the fiery flag launched, then arched. The fat legs remained unscathed.

There was stunned silence from the crowd at the joust. Everyone stared while Barney stood in the middle of the square dodging falling debris.

"Wha' in 'eaven's name are ya doin' up there?" he cried and marched angrily toward the stairs he'd just descended.

"Oops!" Tim muttered.

A moment later an irate Barney stood before him. "Whatcha think yer doin' there? I di'n't give ya 'at thing to destroy the place."

"I'm sorry. I just wanted to see how powerful it was."

"It's a magic wand, fer cryin' out loud. Magic wands are powerful."

"Then why'd you give it to me?"

"Cuz 'at's what I do," Barney said, "No one's ever blown the place apart b'fore. They usually mike li'le bunny rabbits and float tables 'bout rooms and such like."

"I didn't know it did that," Tim explained. "It just sort of started blowing things up."

"Oh, say, young man," someone called to him from the square below.

Tim looked over the stone wall. A man dressed in rich forest green stood there. He sported the customary well-cropped beard and tufts of gray hair that peeked from beneath a forest green velvet cap that rested haphazardly on his head.

"You want me?" Tim called down.

"I say, quite a peashooter you have there, eh?" The thick accent whistled through large, horse-sized teeth. Tim could count them even from where he stood.

"It was an accident," Tim explained a bit sheepishly.

"Could you come down?" the man requested. "I've a proposition for you."

Barney groaned. "Proposition? Me eye."

Tim glanced at Barney. "What kind of proposition?"

Barney spat. "Nothin'," he said and shook his head violently.

Tim couldn't figure out the little guy at all. He decided to go down and see what the green man had to say. "I'll be right down," Tim called.

"Splendid."

Barney stayed at his heels grumbling about little toads and bunny rabbits, but he fell silent when Tim stepped onto the cobbled square. The instant his feet hit the cobbles, he found a large, outstretched hand waiting for him to shake. He did.

"I'm Basil Larch." The man introduced himself with a toothy smile.

"Tim Craft," Tim returned.

"I saw what you did up there."

"I can work to pay for the damage."

Larch laughed loudly. "No, no. Not at all. I always hated the cherub anyway. Would much prefer a cricket bat or such like. I'm a sportsman, you know."

"Are those knights working for you?"

Larch grinned. "About half of them are."

"Who do the other half work for?"

Larch grinned more broadly. "Other people." His arm reached around Tim's shoulder. "Could you show me how that works?" He asked as he tapped the wand.

A caution flag went up in Tim's brain. If he did show him how it worked the man might steal it from him. "I'll make it work. But I won't show you how."

Larch frowned, his front teeth poking his lower lip. "Okay," he said, brows dipping low.

As Tim had moved near the center of the cobblestone square, Barney had remained near the stairs and leaned against a brick wall. A stone vase with unkempt weeds draping over its ragged edges stood near him. Tim stepped away from Larch, aimed the wand at the vase, and hissed, "Creep!"

The vase exploded. Dirt and stone flew everywhere. Barney screamed, ducked and barely avoided the really big pieces. Tim had to laugh at the little guy, but his laughter faded when he noticed another man, draped in a dark robe, his face hidden in shadows, standing off to the side watching him.

"Creep?" Larch said. "You said 'creep'?"

"That's what I said." Tim affirmed. "You have no idea what I *did*."

The man nodded acknowledgment. "Now, for my proposition."

While Barney screeched at him from the stairs, Tim faced Larch. He liked having something people wanted.

"I'd like to pay you a lot of money."

"But money doesn't do me any good . . . "

"What if you wanted to buy something while you were here?" Larch asked, his voice becoming wire thin.

Buy something, Tim thought. What if he was supposed to earn money to buy the formula? This could be fun. "Right. What if?" he said.

"I'd like you to ride for me."

Tim's breath caught. "Against those knights?"

"It could be fun," Larch said as his arm slipped around Tim's shoulder, his eyes stared deeply into Tim's, and his grin became like a Cheshire cat's.

"But that looks dangerous."

"Not with this," Larch's bony finger stroked the wand reverently.

Tim eyed the wand again. It did work pretty well, and he was a reasonably good horseman, though certainly no knight. "How much?"

"A million."

"A million?!"

"Not enough? Two million."

"Dollars?"

"If you wish. I usually just pay in gold."

"Gold?!"

"Not good enough?"

"No. Gold's fine. Real fine."

"Then you'll do it? Wonderful." Larch took Tim's hand and firmly shook it. "It's a deal, then."

"Deal."

The man in the shadows straightened and was looking far more alert now that Tim's and Larch's hands had clasped.

"Well, lad," Larch said as he pulled him along, "let me show you to my tent."

"Tent?"

"Where you'll be dressed. I have the finest dresser in the business."

"Dressed?"

"Armor and the like," Larch explained. "Wonderful armor. Made by elves in Saskatchewan."

"Elves in Saskatchewan?"

"You certainly do have a way of keeping the conversation going, don't you, lad?"

The green tents stood at the near end of the tournament field. A string of muscular horses, roans and blacks, stood flicking flies in back. Tim had never seen such beautiful animals.

"Go into that first tent, there." Larch pointed, then turned away.

Suddenly a knight, green banners flying, galloped in front of Tim. The crowd roared their approval as he headed around the tent, then back toward the tournament field. Tim had difficulty picturing himself astride such a fine animal, looking so well-groomed and so powerful and receiving such applause.

Tim glanced to his right beyond the field to some wagons. Standing beside one of them was the man in the dark cape. Again shadows erased his face. A disquieting feeling swept over Tim. Who was he?

Inside the dimly lit tent a small man slouched in a chair snoring. Dressed from head to toe in green, he had a huge mustache that draped down the sides of his chin and nearly made it to his chest. It fluttered with each thunderous wheeze.

"Mister," Tim called.

The man sputtered but didn't wake. Tim nudged him in the stomach with the wand. The man sputtered again, and this time his eyes sprang open and he leaped to attention. When he saw who it was, though, he slouched again. "What you want?" he asked.

"Mr. Larch told me to come in here and get dressed."

The little man's mustache seemed to straighten at that one. "You?"

"I'm to ride for him."

"You?!" The little man became more incredulous.

Tim thought he ought to feel hurt, but he could understand the man's reaction. Dressing knights with acres of muscles all day long probably jaded him to people with Tim's physique.

"I have this wand," Tim said and lifted the wand feebly.

"Are you sure . . ?"

But the man with the mustache didn't finish. From behind Tim came another voice—a wonderfully familiar voice.

"Hello, Tim."

He turned to see Sonya. His heart dropped to his shoes.

As beautiful as ever, she wore a lush, crimson gown that cascaded over her shoulders to the sawdust floor. Large, soft eyes searched his face as her blush pink lips smiled.

"Sonya?" Tim gushed with excitement. But just as quickly his excitement dampened. From some forgotten corner of his brain, Kelly whispered, "She's a 'toon.'" He peered at Sonya more closely. She was a cartoon—a perfect cartoon. There were no blemishes, no wrinkles, no texture to her skin. Although her eyes sparkled wonderfully, there was no depth to them.

"What's the matter, Tim?" Sonya became perplexed.

He shuffled reluctantly. Then whispered, "You're not real."

Sonya smiled, lips pink and soft. "What's real, Tim? Real is what we see, what we feel. Do you feel this?" She brought a warm hand up and brushed it softly across his cheek.

The electric thrill surged through him.

"Is that real?" she asked.

He hesitated but then smiled. "It's good to see you."

"It's wonderful to see you." Her smile faded just a bit. "I understand you have a marvelous new toy."

"Toy?"

"The wand," she said pointing at what he held in his hand.

"A little guy, Barney, gave it to me."

"It's very powerful." Sonya stared at it.

"You've never seen one before?" Tim asked.

"We've seen them. But only to make bunny rabbits and toads—not stone bellies explode."

"I guess I know how to do that."

"Would you show me?" Sonya asked.

The man with the mustache grunted, "'E ain't got time. This 'ere's Larch's tent and I'm to dress 'im."

"But you're already dressed," Sonya said to Tim.

"I'm riding for Mr. Larch against the other knights," Tim told her.

"You are?" Sonya looked hurt. "Some of those knights are my knights."

"But how . . . "

"My daddy's rich," she explained. "You wouldn't hurt my knights, would you?"

Tim swallowed very hard and repeated, "Your knights?"

The mustache shook an angry finger, "Now see 'ere. Sir Larch employed that 'ere bloke . . ."

"Quiet!" Sonya snapped, then turned soft eyes on Tim. "You don't want to hurt my knights—or hurt me, do you?" An idea struck her. "What if you rode for me?"

"You?" Tim swallowed hard again.

"Yes, me." Sonya glared, but then softened again.

"But," began the mustache, "Sir Larch is payin' 'im a lot o' money."

A finger circled the edge of his ear, "You don't care about money, do you, Tim? You know Jesus, don't you, Tim?"

"Money? Jesus?" Tim backed up a step, his mind at war with his heart, and both at war with the knot in his stomach. "But I promised . . . "

"Promised?" Sonya cooed. "Everyone knows a promise doesn't mean anything here. Did you spit and step on it after you promised?"

"Well," Tim thought, "no, I didn't."

Sonya looked greatly relieved. "Well, then, you didn't promise. You only said you would."

"Really?" Tim began to feel relieved, too.

"Good. That's settled," Sonya took him by the arm. "Let's get you to my tent, and we'll get you into some beautiful clothes." She frowned at the little man with the mustache. "Who wants to look like a tree, anyway?"

"You can't do this." The little man turned as red as Sonya's dress. "I'll tell Sir Larch. And there's no telling what he'll do."

Sonya eyed the little man with contempt as she led Tim from the tent. "He'll lump it, that's what he'll do."

Tim definitely liked the adventure of riding in a joust, but he didn't like the idea of promising and then going back on it, even if he hadn't spit and stepped on it. He did like the idea of riding for Sonya. But he didn't like the idea of being manipulated. And another thought was forming that he didn't like —he didn't like blowing people up, even raging knights.

He especially didn't like the fact that the man in the shadows was watching when he and Sonya stepped from the tent and walked toward her bigger, red one. Tim thought he knew who it was, and he wished he would go away.

And what he really, really, *really* didn't like was the Cadillac ambulance that sat near the tent, with the white-clad attendants playing cards on the hood. He had the feeling it would be he, Tim Craft, who interrupted their game next.

CHAPTER 17

The beastly howl faded but soon returned. The sound seemed to seep from the very stone surrounding Kelly, then echo in front of and behind her. Although it didn't grow in volume and it did fade in and out, it never ceased.

Was it Harve?

She listened for a human inflection, an imperfection in the horrific strain that pointed to Harve as the source. But it never wavered—it remained mournfully pure.

The cave itself didn't change much from turn to turn—black, obsidian walls, boulders that lined them like teeth, and sand beneath her feet. Now and then drops of water plopped and joined the eerie echoes. At one point a small waterfall cascaded and splashed playfully in a crystalline hollow.

Then a bat flew by.

Kelly froze. It came from up ahead of her, fluttered overhead, then, as she spun to watch it, disappeared around a bend.

Kelly couldn't think of anything she hated more than bats. Maybe rats, but bats were right up there. She listened. In a National Geographic special on TV she'd heard what a bat cave sounds like—the incessant chirping and beating of wings.

She heard none of that—only the ghoulish howl.

Maybe she'd chosen the wrong fork.

Maybe the howl was a warning from the Lord and maybe the bat was his way of tapping her hard on the shoulder.

Maybe it wasn't Harve up there after all, and her worst

nightmare was about to leap frothing at the mouth from beyond the next turn.

Maybe she ought to just turn back. The fork wasn't that far back. Maybe she was at the football game, and fourteen inches of snow were about to dump all over her. Isn't it better just to admit a mistake and correct it?

Yep, that's what she'd do. A wave of relief broke over her as she turned and made her way quickly to the previous turn. But the moment she was around it, relief vanished. Blocking the cave and her retreat was a set of rusty steel jail bars. They were anchored securely in the ceiling and floor, and hanging from the ceiling just before them, its black leathery wings wrapped around like a miniature Dracula, was the bat.

Kelly stood like stone for a long moment.

Then, with her insides knotted and the bat never out of sight, she stepped slowly backward until she made it back around the bend. She took a huge breath, said a quick prayer, and continued toward whatever awaited her.

Tim stood beside a large, brown speckled horse with red banners strapped all over it. His outfit was red as well—red top, red leggings, red hat, red plume. The only thing not red was his armor. A red-clad attendant, who looked remarkably like the green-clad attendant he'd just left, helped him with dutiful resolve. And it wasn't easy. The armor was built for large, muscular knights. When Tim put it on, his body seemed like a clapper inside a very large bell. The neck hole was so large that at one point it slipped down over his shoulders and pinned his arms to his sides. "Can't 'ave 'at," the attendant moaned and stuffed Tim's shirt with rags.

As he waited, Tim detected a definite pattern to all the screaming from the crowd. First, an eruption of yells and screams signaled the start of the joust. Then, as hooves thundered toward one another, there was a long, crescendoing roar. A quick gasp was followed by a short, hopeful cheer. Then came a rapid-fire mix of cheers and "oohs." Now and then there was a collective "ouch," and finally one side would send up a mournful "ah" while a deafening cheer rose up from the other. There was silence for a few minutes before it started all over again.

"Bloodthirsty bunch," Tim observed as he tried to figure out how he was going to mount such a huge animal.

"We do love our games," the attendant said with a deeply satisfied smile.

A thought struck Tim. "How do you aim this thing when you're riding a horse?" he asked.

"I don't," the attendant grunted. "I don't ride 'orses. I don't aim wands, and I don't blow things up by yellin' at 'em."

Out of the corner of Tim's eye he saw something very large and very green enter the tent. Sir Larch!

"Tim, m'lad." Larch sounded as if he was using great control.

Tim turned. "Yes, Sir Larch." He spoke with immense respect, nearly reverence.

"Why are you dressed in that hideous color?" More restraint, but the binds were wearing thin.

"Red?" Tim asked sheepishly.

"Why aren't you in the glorious green we all love so much?"

"Green?" Tim asked more sheepishly still.

"And you must have wandered from my tent."

"Your tent?"

"Tim," more control, this time salted with a deep bond of friendship, "you promised. We shook hands. I said I would pay you great sums of money."

"Money?"

Sir Larch exploded, "Yes, money!" The explosion became a molten eruption. "Why are you *here*?"

Sonya suddenly appeared at the tent entrance. "Because he's decided to ride for me," she told Larch, looking very businesslike. "Haven't you, Tim?"

Tim, head bowed slightly, nodded. "Yes, I have."

"But you promised," Larch declared.

"But he didn't spit and step on it, did you, Tim?"

Tim shook his head meekly.

Larch's brows screwed up. "He didn't what?"

"Now, Sir Larch," Sonya said brusquely, "you run along and leave Tim alone. He has a joust for which to prepare. Don't you, Tim?"

Tim nodded again, even more meekly, "For which . . . uh, yes. I have a joust to . . . uh . . . for which to prepare for . . . which . . ."

Larch tapped his foot and repeatedly slapped a green glove he'd been carrying into his other hand. "Well, that's how it is, is it? We'll just see about this." He paused. "For this you'll face my most powerful knight. I've been letting him rest for a while. All that killing does something to a person. But now his rest is over. You'll face Sir Cruncher. Did you hear me?" Larch pushed his face at Tim. "Sir Cruncher!"

"Well," said Sonya, "that is good news. Today we get to see exploding Cruncher." And she laughed.

Larch stormed from the tent, and Sonya immediately softened and moved toward Tim. He found himself taking a small step away from her. "Don't worry, Tim. He's all bluster."

"Bluster?" muttered Tim.

"Now, you relax for a few minutes," she said as she patted him encouragingly on his chest. "I'll stick my head in when its time. Maybe you ought to go out back and practice with that wand of yours."

Tim nodded. "Maybe."

"Don't worry. It'll be all right."

Tim nodded again. "Maybe," he said, his heart heavy. But after she left he realized he'd come too far to back out now. Feeling the wand's smoothness, he decided she was right. Maybe he ought to give it just one more try.

He stepped out into the sunlight. The crowd's roar crescendoed, and hooves thundered as he looked for a target. He saw a water jug on a bench not too far away. He pointed, imagined holding the wand steady on horseback, and half-heartedly growled, "Creep!" The jug burst, and a thick spray of water splashed several feet in all directions.

"Hey, kid," Tim heard, and from the shadows behind the jug stepped the figure in the dark cape. He was sopping wet—and angry.

CHAPTER 18

Another bat suddenly flapped overhead and disappeared behind Kelly. For just an instant the cave's ever-present glow caught the fire in its eyes, and she was sure she saw a glint of fangs. Curious, she stepped back around the last bend. Sure enough, another set of bars blocked her retreat, and the new bat hung before them like the other.

She didn't like being controlled like this, but she had no alternative but to submit. She listened again to the hideous, distant shriek and continued walking.

The cave made another turn, and the howl grew louder. After yet another turn, the character of the cave changed. Instead of the narrow black walls, Kelly's path broadened and became more room-like; a sparkle of quartz shimmered on the wall, casting an eerie green and yellow tint on the stone.

"Hi," a voice said, startling her.

A shadow moved from behind a boulder—a short, pear-shaped shadow. "Harve? That you?"

"I've been waiting for you," the dwarf said, happy his wait was over.

The howl swelled again from up ahead.

"So it's not you?"

"Not me where?"

"Doing the howling."

"Can't say that it is," Harve said and stepped into what light there was and smiled at her.

"What do you think it is?" Kelly asked, the unearthly quality of the sound becoming more significant now.

"Don't know. It does sound spooky though."

"We can't go back."

"Because of the jail bars?" Harve asked casually. "No. We can either stay here or go forward."

"We can't stay here," Kelly stated more to herself than to Harve. "I've got to find something."

"Then we go forward." Harve nodded with determination.

"Right," Kelly said, continuing with some reluctance. "Forward."

Around the next bend, the cry became particularly mournful, as if it were rooted in a bed of severe, soul-rending pain. Kelly winced.

"Why are you here, Harve?" she asked in a feeble attempt to shake the sound from her head.

"Why anywhere? A conditional branch," Harve stated.

"What's that?"

"You know. 'If girl is in cave, then Harve appears.' Or 'If girl washes up on beach, Harve hides behind rock.' Computer language. A condition occurs, and Harve is told to do something."

Kelly nodded. "You just wait for the right thing to happen."

"And I pop up. Can't do it before, only after. Some life, huh?" Harve sighed sounding depressed.

"Better than waiting for some beast to jump you." Then a thought struck. "Do you feel pain?"

Harve pondered that for a second, "No, not really. I say 'ouch' and grab my arm sometimes. But that's about all."

"So I could send you on ahead, and if there's a monster it wouldn't hurt you." That idea appealed to Kelly.

"No pain," Have said, walking beside her, "but I have a definite aversion to being ripped apart. No, you're on your own with monsters."

"Well, then, if it wasn't to save me, what condition brought you here?" Kelly asked, baffled.

"I gotta be somewhere," Harve stated. "Actually that's not true. I don't gotta be anywhere. I just come and go." He frowned. "What a life!"

The sound changed. Kelly wasn't sure when she noticed

it, but now she detected a certain human quality. Instead of seeming to rise like a vapor from the very depths of hell, it now seemed to come from a human throat. Tempered and battered by the cavern walls, it still sounded frightening. But now it was human—a human in incredible agony.

If someone was in pain . . .

"I think we need to hurry," Kelly said. "Someone might be hurt up there."

She didn't wait for Harve to reply but began to run. Harve fell behind, his little legs unable to keep up with Kelly.

Suddenly she rounded a corner, and everything changed. Although she was still underground, she broke into a huge cavern. The ceiling reached high above her to a gigantic dome. A round skylight opened to the outer world and sent down a bright shaft of light that pierced the cave's darkness. Stalactites, great spikes of rock, reached from the ceiling, some down to the floor, forming huge frothy columns of stone.

Kelly's path led off to the right, and she could have continued on but she didn't.

A canyon cut the room in two. When Kelly peered into it, she could detect no bottom, only endless black. On the other side of the canyon, her back draped grotesquely over a rock, lay a girl dressed in jeans and a dark blue ski jacket. Her hair matted over her face, and the rock under her head was bloodstained. Her cries of pain were every bit as horrible up close as they had been in the cave.

Harve ran up beside Kelly.

"Do you know her?" Kelly asked him, her eyes fixed on the girl. "It looks like her back's broken."

"I can't see her face from here," Harve said, leaning as close to the canyon as he dared.

"If she's make-believe, I don't have time to help."

"I don't think she's from around here," Harve finally said.

Kelly called out to her, "Are you a 'toon?"

The girl replied with a heart-wrenching scream of agony.

"I can't stand this." Kelly frantically looked about for a way over the canyon. There was none that she could see. The canyon was a sheer drop to nowhere. "Why are you here?" she called to the injured girl.

The girl raised her head just an inch and tried to turn toward them, but the movement must have been excruciating for she lay back suddenly and burst into tears. The shaking caused by her crying seemed to intensify her pain, and she broke into a heart-stopping wail.

"I saw her face," Harve announced with a hint of triumph. "I really think I saw her face. She's not from the computer."

"Then why is she here?" Kelly asked more to herself than to Harve.

"I don't know." Harve also began to sound frantic.

"Can you do something?" Kelly asked. "Jump tall buildings in a single bound or something? You can do anything in animation. Can't you get across this stupid little canyon?"

"No. I don't do things like that—tall buildings in a single bound? Wow!"

Kelly anxiously wrung her hands and gnawed at her lower lip. "No, I don't have time to help. I can't help. I don't even know why she's here." Kelly turned and paced to her left, then to her right. "I have to keep going. I have to."

The girl cried out again. The pain in the cry, the agony that spilled into the air washed over Kelly.

"You're right, you know," said another voice—a man's voice. It came from behind Kelly in the cave.

She turned. A darkly dressed man stood there, his face buried in shadows. His black cape glistened as if wet.

"Who are you?" Kelly would have taken a step back but feared the canyon.

"It doesn't matter," said the man stepping from the shadows. In his forties, the man's eyes were deeply set, his shoulders broad and muscular under the cape.

"You're wet?"

"No time to explain that—that stupid brother of yours," the man spat.

"Tim? You know where Tim is?"

"That doesn't matter either," the man said as he eyed his watch. "You have to get going. There's no time for these diversions."

"But she's hurt."

"The world is hurt. The world needs that formula, and one girl with a silly little injury shouldn't stand in the way—"

"How do you know about the formula?"

"Everybody in here knows about the formula. And everybody wants you to find it."

"What formula?" Harve said with a shrug. "And I don't care if you find it or not."

"Shut up, shrimp," the dark man snapped.

Another cry of agony rose from the girl across the canyon.

"By the time you take care of her—even if you can find a way—it'll be too late."

"Too late for what?" Kelly asked.

"Just too late." The man eyed his watch again and took out a small calculator-sized box. He glanced at it for a moment, then said, "I've got to go do something. Take the advice of someone who's on your side—forget her and get going."

Kelly stepped toward the man. "You're Hammond Helbert, aren't you?"

But the man didn't hear her. He was already gone.

"I'm not sure I like him much," Harve said.

Kelly turned back toward the girl. "He might be right."

Another cry. This one seemed to have a word trapped in it—"Help."

Kelly took a deep breath. "I can't just leave her like this. The Lord wouldn't want me to leave her in pain."

"But what about the world?" Harve asked.

"God's a loving God. He wouldn't ask me to make a choice like that. He'll make sure I can do both. Come on. We have to figure out how to get across this canyon."

CHAPTER 19

The time had come for Tim to perform, and there'd be no backing out. Mounting the brown speckled charger hadn't been easy. He'd had to climb stairs, heave himself so that his belly lay across the saddle—and then he slid off the other side. The red-clad dresser had grunted in disbelief. But Tim was astride the horse now, and although the mount was massive, Tim had been riding horses since he was just out of diapers, so he eased the animal around comfortably.

A joust was in progress. The "cheer" cycle had reached the mix of cheers and "ahs" as the ground battle progressed and weapons battered armor and shield.

A little while ago one of the knights had broken the rules. He'd produced an automatic rifle and peppered his opponent with machine-gun fire. He was fined for unsportsmanlike conduct. It delayed the games for a while, and Tim found himself hoping they would be called off entirely. But they weren't.

It seemed that the only escape was to give up. He could do it with just a quick push of his palm. But that would mean defeat for everyone.

If he could just stay in the saddle and blow Sir Cruncher out of his, it would all be over and he could continue his quest.

The final cheer erupted from the green side. Before Tim knew it the ambulance, siren wailing, sped out to pick up the loser's remains. He had hoped that Sonya would come back to give him some of that moral support she was so good at, but she hadn't reappeared.

Tim's horse's name was emblazoned in white majestic swirls below his neck and across his chest—*Ralph. Strange name for a horse,* Tim thought. He suddenly heard a sound from the crowd that he hadn't heard before. A reverent hush, followed by a warm, appreciative "ah." Tim nudged Ralph forward to see the cause—and immediately he wished he hadn't.

Sir Cruncher rode gallantly onto the field. He was huge—a medieval Goliath. His horse made Ralph look like a pony, and Sir Cruncher, stiff in the saddle, added another five feet. His armor glistened in the sunlight, and the total package, horse and knight, reminded Tim of a locomotive.

Tim leaned forward in his saddle and sucked in his breath. He eyed his wand. No way could that little stick put even a dent in that guy.

Of course, David probably thought the same thing about the five stones he'd chosen when he faced Goliath.

No, thought Tim, *he didn't. David was on the Lord's mission and his faith and his strength came from that.*

Tim cringed inside. In all honesty, he doubted he could say the same.

Suddenly the loudspeaker blared, "In green, riding Mac-Truck, is Sir Cruncher."

A frenzied cheer went up from the green side and from half the other side—a patchwork quilt of colors, red being a small section in the upper right.

"Aboard Ralph is Tim."

The announcement didn't sound at all impressive. The weak cheer sounded even less so.

Tim eased Ralph to the starting position at the end of a long railing. MacTruck and Cruncher stood about a football field away, on the other side of the railing. Even at that distance the knight looked massive. He leaned over and grabbed a lance from an aide. He hefted it like kindling, then lowered the visor on his helmet and leveled the lance's point at Tim.

Tim glanced at his wand again—such a feeble weapon—

even if it had burned flags and blown flower vases to rubble. But then another troubling thought struck—all those objects had been things. Now he was going to be aiming it at a person—virtual murder. He didn't like the sound of that. Maybe he could think of it as virtual self-defense . . .

"Well, m' lad," said the red dresser, "this is it."

"I sure hope this works," Tim muttered. He had no more time to ponder deep moral issues. He had a knight to blow up.

"Oh, I'm sure it will work fine. And don't worry about the money you gave up. I'm sure Miss Sonya will share the winnings."

The bugle blew. Cheers rose from either side. Sir Cruncher spurred his horse forward.

"Winnings?" Tim's face screwed up questioningly.

"Sure. She's got alo' o' money wagered on you."

"This is to win a bet!?"

"You better hurry, lad. I don't want that fella too close to 'ere," said the red dresser as he slapped Ralph on the rump.

"A lousy bet?" Tim cried. But there was no time to think about bets or how stupid he felt. The green locomotive, its lance leveled at Tim's heart, chugged relentlessly his way.

And chug he did. MacTruck's tree trunk legs reached out and grabbed acres of earth and thundered deafeningly. Cruncher leaned low, and his lance a horrible extension of the fury that surrounded him. He came fast—very fast.

With Ralph churning below him, Tim tried to muster composure enough to aim. If he fired the wand quickly there might still be a chance, but Ralph's large, bouncing back and the shock of hooves pounding the ground afforded little opportunity to even get the wand pointed in the right general direction.

In desperation, hoping something miraculous might happen, Tim pointed the stick forward and shouted, "Creep!" The post supporting the judges' stand exploded, the stand collapsed, and judges rolled everywhere like colorful billiard balls.

Tim yelled, "Bird brain!" and a covered wagon with a

huge sheriff's star painted on the side erupted, the canvas ablaze.

MacTruck kept coming, the knight aboard him shrouded in the dirt thrown up by his thunderous hooves.

Tim pointed and yelled, "Geek!" He missed again and hit the green side grandstand supports. As it collapsed people rolled out like green BBs.

It was no use. Within seconds that point would slam into him. Within seconds, computer-generated graphics or not, something terrible was going to happen. Maybe he'd even die. Maybe the shock to his heart would be too much.

Tim braced for the inevitable, one eye closed, the other squinting.

And then it all stopped. Everything. The sound, the blurred figure ready to push his weapon deep into Tim's heart, the collapsing grandstand, the judges shaking their fists at him, the burning wagon, the laughing people in the other grandstand. Everything and everyone was frozen in time and space, ready to begin again, but only a frenzied painting now.

Yet Tim could still move.

"I can't believe you went through with this," a befuddled, yet angry voice said.

Tim turned. Standing on the ground only a few feet from Tim's frozen horse was the man in the dark cape.

"You're just like your sister. Don't you know you're running out of time?"

"My sister? Is she still. . . ?"

"She won't be for long. I can't believe you two. The world's about to end, and you're playing Dungeons and Dragons here."

"Who are you? Wait—I know . . ."

"I'm Hammond. Congratulations," the man said sarcastically. "But that's neither here nor there, kid. You've got to get busy!"

"Why are you following me?"

"I'm trying to keep you on track—and I seem to be failing miserably. I can't believe you actually got on that horse and faced King Kong there. But I came back, and there you were about to get killed. You *can* get killed, you know. My brother made it that way. For me, I suspect."

"He knew you'd take the formula and blackmail the world with it."

"Me? He's crazy. I'm a small-time thief. He was the crackpot. Being a genius, I could see the danger of what he was doing. I want that formula destroyed as much as you do. I came here to help. And what do I find?"

Tim glanced up at the charging MacTruck. "What happened here?"

"Everything stopped," Hammond answered matter-of-factly. He leaned back like an artist admiring his work, then said, "Boy, I love this stuff. Knights and all. Swinging big swords. Just makes the ol' blood pump faster."

"I'm not so fond of it. I thought I was going to die."

"You were. Maybe still are." Hammond's eyes looked out from under furled, serious brows. "I've been roaming around this little world my brother concocted for months. I've learned a few things. This, here, is a debug option."

"You correct the program this way?"

"Sure. You can stop everything, work with one or two characters, or items, then start things up again."

"How'd he write all this?" Tim asked suddenly in awe of it all.

"He didn't. The computer did. My brother wrote an overseer program that writes—or generates—the actual code that makes everything work—in real time—right now. It's quite an accomplishment." Hammond sounded respectful too. "And it's a shame—" His awe faded to agitation again. "We don't have much time. And you guys are getting waylaid . . ."

"What's a shame?"

"Trust me. All this is going to evaporate very soon. And with it will go the formula if we don't pick up the pace. There is no time to waste."

"Why will it evaporate?" Tim asked.

"It dies when my brother dies. That was his protection against me. And believe me, those comas don't last forever—four days, tops. He's been out for three."

"Then let's go."

"We can't," Hammond stated. "We can't leave this scene. It has to be played out."

Hammond suddenly grabbed the wand and with a quick motion snapped it. The smooth limb now hung limp in two pieces.

"What'd you do that for?"

"My protection. You're wild with that thing."

"A little," Tim admitted.

Suddenly Hammond grabbed Tim's leg and lifted him easily onto his horse.

"Okay, I'm going to start this thing again. Do what comes naturally."

"Naturally?"

Hammond groaned impatiently, stepped back and snapped his fingers.

Between heartbeats the thunder, the blur of the advancing knight, the deafening screams of the crowd, the angry shouts of the judges—everything returned. And Tim's panic definitely returned, especially after he looked down at his broken wand. If it looked feeble and ineffective before, it looked doubly so now.

The point of the lance loomed only a few waning feet from his heart now, and in spite of the frenzied pounding of MacTruck's legs, the point remained steady as ice.

What came naturally came.

Tim ducked.

He pushed himself to the side of the saddle, hugged the huge animal, and the lance only nicked his ear. There was a sharp shock of pain there, but the fact that he could still feel it was all that really counted.

The crowd booed and hissed.

But that mattered little to Tim. He was still alive. Ralph seemed a bit ashamed of his rider and came to a screeching halt. This launched Tim out of the saddle to land face down on the ground.

Everything ached as he rolled over to see MacTruck with Sir Cruncher still aboard saunter up to him. When they hovered above him like a green thundercloud, the lance point dropped to his chest. The weight of it alone would probably kill him.

Tim could hardly breathe.

Suddenly something very sharp and very quick whipped over him and cut the lance out of the Cruncher's hand; the point fell to the side.

Hammond stood there, a large sword clutched in his hand.

"Don't take the boy," he growled. "What will his death add to your honor? Take me on, Sir Cruncher."

Hammond didn't have to ask twice.

MacTruck reared, its huge hooves rising up like waffle irons ready to make breakfast out of Hammond. Hammond spun away and in doing so diverted the knight's attention away from Tim.

Tim didn't wait to see the outcome. He sprang to his feet and ran smack into the arms of ten angry judges, two raging sheriffs, and one scowling Sonya.

"Hi, Sonya," Tim greeted. "Anything else I can help you with?"

Her scowl deepened to rage.

It was the green Sir Larch who stepped up behind the sheriffs and pronounced his fate, "To the dungeon."

As Hammond boldly fought the Cruncher, now with mace and shield, Tim was carried off, none too gently, to the dungeon.

Aptly named, it looked like a movie dungeon: gray rock walls, straw strewn everywhere, torture devices standing about, a rack to lounge on in the corner, bars on the little window in the very thick door that slammed shut behind Tim, locking out the mob that was calling for his head and the faint rush of the crowd still hissing in the distance. Hammond must have been holding his own against the gorilla.

Devastation settled over Tim like vultures over a fallen animal. It picked at him, beat him. He'd failed. He always failed. If there was a decision to make he'd make the wrong one.

Now he'd let a cartoon girl send him to a dungeon—a dungeon built by a genius probably to hold the non-Christian contenders for his formula.

He'd been found wanting. And this was where he was to end up.

Tim shivered. A cold chill, as cold as he'd ever experienced, crawled up his spine.

Defeated, he sat in the dungeon's only chair—rough-hewn with thick leather straps to sit and lean against, next to an ancient wooden table in the corner.

Planting his elbows on the table, Tim buried his head in his hands. About to cry—something he hadn't done since he was a young boy—he saw what his elbows rested upon. A Bible.

He almost turned away, but something told him to open it. The cover was thick ancient leather, and the backing creaked as he picked a point far back in the New Testament. He flipped a few of the yellowed pages and stopped at 2 Corinthians 7. He began to read. Words that had never meant much to him suddenly meant everything, "Godly sorrow leading to repentance," he whispered over and over again.

"Repentance," he muttered, "forgiveness."

He prayed.

He had done wrong. He'd allowed his own wants to overshadow the Lord's word. He'd fooled himself into thinking he was doing the right things when inside he knew he wasn't. He'd misused the wand. Calling people names in anger like he'd done with the wand was just like murder. Jesus said so in the Sermon on the Mount. He flipped over to Matthew 5 and read Jesus' command not to be angry with others. Tim had been drawn into something he knew from the beginning was wrong by someone he knew from the beginning wasn't right for him. "Sonya doesn't belong to you," he finally admitted to the Lord.

His amen had a hopeless ring to it.

But the moment he uttered it, he felt something strange—an inner strength. At first just a surge of optimism, it quickly became a haven of peace, then it became physical. His muscles came alive, and his heart pumped more fervently. New resolve swept through him. He was God's child, and he was going to start behaving like it.

He stood and looked around him. The dungeon was still there, the rack was still there, the bars were still there. But suddenly things changed. The front door exploded and through the dust, Barney appeared.

"You ready?" he asked as he waved a new wand in front of him.

"Ready?"

Barney shook his head disgustedly but recovered. "I hear you repented. The true sign of a Christian. Follow me. We got a formula to find."

"Really?"

"Come on. You're quite articulate, you know."

Tim quickly followed Barney through the dust out into the corridor lit by a single shaft of light. "You're using the wand," Tim observed.

"'Hallelujah' works too," Barney said, waving the wand. "At the right times, that is."

"Where are we going?"

"To the Thistle," Barney said with great reverence.

"The Thistle?" Tim repeated.

"Maybe you ought to just follow along and keep your clever patter to yourself."

Tim eagerly took his position behind Barney.

CHAPTER 20

Harve saw the bridge first. It was a rainbow of rock that leaped from high on the cavern wall far to the left of the cave's exit, over the bottomless canyon, to the other side. The approach to the bridge was ragged and punctuated by sheer drops. The climb would be dangerous.

But none of that mattered. The girl across the canyon was in agony, and if Kelly could do anything to help, she would.

"Well, here goes," Kelly said, her eyes searching the jagged, rocky steps immediately ahead.

Harve said, "I wish I could help."

"You could pray."

"I could and I shall." Harve nodded fervently.

Kelly took a deep breath, said a little prayer of her own, then started her ascent.

Hammond eyed the splintered remains of the dungeon door and cursed beneath his breath, "The idiot must have stumbled on a way out—an explosive way out." He stepped inside and immediately saw the open Bible. He grabbed it angrily and threw it across the room. The pages fluttered violently as it landed in a pile of straw.

Hammond took a small visual display terminal from beneath his cape and typed in Tim's name. A translucent cube appeared and a dot blinked inside it. Below the cube 63 zeros and ones appeared in several lines across the bottom of the display.

"That's a new one," Hammond mumbled and pushed a key marked "destination address." The display blinked indicating the address of 63 zeros and ones had been stored. "Well, here goes." He grunted and pressed a key marked "leap." He disappeared.

A rock under Kelly's foot came loose, and she slid back a few feet. Quickly regaining her balance, she recovered the distance. The rocks presented a natural stairway, so the going was easier than she first thought it would be. But another problem cropped up. The higher she climbed, the more fearsome the drop. When she was about halfway up to the bridge a fear she didn't know existed kicked in. Suddenly she looked down, and her heart caught, her muscles locked, and she felt strangely dizzy. Instinctively she knew what it was—vertigo.

Maybe that's where her fear of flying came from. Maybe when that door closed and her mind realized she was about to climb, it remembered the fear and brought the panic.

Why hadn't she felt it when she was being carried along by the wind? She'd been a lot higher then. Maybe she had felt safe in the palm of the wind, and then she remembered the panic she'd felt when she encountered a bump or air pocket.

Now there was no palm to rest in.

Then she smiled. Sure there was—God's palm. He'd brought her here; he'd see her through.

She shook the tension away and continued.

As the cries from below dulled, Kelly finally reached the bridge. Maybe thirty feet in length, it was about a yard in width at the beginning, but then narrowed in the middle to a foot or so. There were no railings. Although crossing the first part would be easy, the middle would be tough. She remembered trying to walk a rail fence back home. Although narrower, it was also much closer to the ground. She'd fallen.

"Of course," she groaned, "I may not have to worry about falling, the middle might just collapse." At that moment she regretted every Snickers candy bar she'd ever eaten.

She glanced down again.

The vertigo returned. Dizziness swept over her, and she fell back against the cliff wall. With heart pounding, she breathed deeply until it passed. If she was going to make it across, she'd have to keep eyes ahead.

The cries from below became more insistent. Again the girl screamed as if a surge of agony had blazed through her.

Balanced carefully, heart thundering, Kelly took her first step, then her second. A wedge of rock slipped under her and she grabbed air for balance. After wobbling for a moment, she took another step, then another. The bridge narrowed. Kelly's arms went out for balance, her eyes straight ahead. One step at a time—one in front of the other. She felt like a tightrope walker. She wobbled—eyes fixed ahead. Her toes felt the surface—another step, then another.

Suddenly her worst fears materialized. She felt the rock behind her give way. She leaped forward, just in time to see the entire middle of the bridge behind her collapse. Landing on her feet, she wobbled and fell to her knees as great chunks of stone fell into the black canyon. She heard them shatter and rain against the canyon walls. She'd landed where the bridge widened, and the rock held firmly beneath her. She looked back. The bridge was no longer a bridge—a gaping hole would keep Harve on the other side.

"Sorry, Harve," she called.

Harve shrugged a response from his perch on a rock. His little legs kicking idly. "That's okay," he called back.

It was only then that Kelly realized she was safely on the other side. Quickly getting to her feet, she started the climb down to the cavern floor. This side of the canyon was broader, and the descent easy.

The cries from the girl were more insistent. Perhaps her condition had worsened, and she was now in greater pain. Kelly tossed away whatever caution remained and ran as quickly as she could.

Reaching the cavern floor, Kelly scrambled toward the girl. As she approached her, she saw that the girl's long auburn hair was matted with blood and her back was bent unnaturally over the rock. She must have fallen a great distance—maybe even from the skylight above.

Kelly immediately knelt and with the most soothing, most encouraging voice she could manage, she said, "It's okay now. We're going to make this better if we can."

The girl turned to her with tortured eyes, and the matted hair fell away from her face.

Kelly couldn't believe her eyes. It was as if she were looking in a mirror—at herself. The girl in agony, the girl with the broken back was Kelly Craft. "It's me," Kelly whispered, and for one horrible moment she was looking into a tortuous future—the pain that accompanied the blood became her pain in some time to come. The thought was chilling. "It's me," she said again.

"I know," Harve said, appearing next to her. "I told you she wasn't from here."

"But it's me. Why is it me?" Kelly brushed the hair away tenderly. A thankful smile slipped over the girl's face.

"It must be for some reason," Harve said, placing a compassionate hand on the girl's forehead.

Kelly wasn't sure what to do. "Is there water around here anywhere? Look, over there. A little pool. Harve, get me some water and we'll clean me up. I'm not sure whether we should move me or not . . . hey! What are you doing over here?"

"I jumped over," Harve said. "I can do that when you're over here."

"What do you mean 'I can do that when you're over here'? Why couldn't you do that over there?"

"When the conditions are right, I can do most anything," Harve explained.

Kelly just sighed and shook her head. "Get the water," she ordered.

That's when the Kelly on the boulder smiled up at her and spoke. "There's no need for that now. You loved me as yourself." And Kelly's image, the one draped painfully across the rock, faded away.

"I don't understand," a very confused Kelly said. She

stood over the rock, and all evidence that her "twin" had ever existed—the blood, the strands of hair—vanished.

"Kelly Craft." Her name came from above. She looked up and saw a man's huge face looking down at her—round with a double chin, hook nose, and eyes set deeply beneath bushy brows. The face covered the whole ceiling.

"I'm Matthew Helbert and there may be very little time to explain," the face said. "You must move quickly. I must assume the worst—the reason you're here. I have determined that you are a Christian and will do the right thing. VR occupant search indicates that my brother is present—probably chasing you—certainly up to no good.

"Something else saddens me. Indications from my brain wave monitor show that I am dying. I hoped I would never take the conditional branch to these words, but I have. When I die everything stops in VR, so there is no time to lose. Harve will be your guide. I modeled him from a dear friend of mine. If you see my brother, run from him. VR will do the rest. If you come to a device, use it—this is a time to trust VR. I'm afraid I've been responsible for something terrible for this conditional branch to be taken, but I designed it for just this occasion. May the Lord of heaven and earth be with you, even in here."

The face disappeared.

Kelly turned to Harve, who turned to Kelly.

"You heard the man," Kelly said.

"A dear friend," Harve said, then took a moment to ponder, "Hmm, you'd think he'd give a dear friend more of a life than this. Come on, Kelly. We've got ground to cover."

Tim and Barney ran from corridor to corridor, building to building, room to room, through this secret passage and that one. Finally, after nearly stumbling down what seemed to be an endless stairway, they burst through a door and found themselves tumbling from the castle.

It was there, with the dark stones at their back, that Matthew Helbert appeared to them. Although they did not know it, he said the exact same thing to them that he had said to Kelly, except that it was Barney who'd be leading Tim.

Tim found the warning about the intruder extremely real. Hammond still roamed about. He hadn't been vanquished by the Cruncher, and he'd probably be showing up again soon.

"Where to, Barn?" Tim asked.

Barney eyed him as if evaluating the boy's stamina. Then he stood on his head and said, "I know some shortcuts. But I'm not sure yer up to 'em."

"I'm up to anything now," Tim said, renewed energy surging through him.

"Well, okay. But you gotta stay close."

"Let's go."

The castle sat on a rocky crag, so their first challenge was to climb down the side of the mountain. When terrain permitted, they ran, but usually they took it only one step at a time.

When they'd gone what seemed about a hundred yards, Barney turned toward the rocky face. "Follow me."

"Where?" Tim asked.

But Barney was already gone. Tim quickly moved to where Barney had stood, and just as suddenly he slipped through a crack in the rock and found himself sliding at breakneck speed down a gravel-covered slide. Tim twisted and turned with the slide and tried to determine where he was going. He couldn't. After a few seconds, he just decided to let things happen.

He picked up speed, then the slide climbed for just a bit and slowed him down, but soon he was going faster again. Though at first exhilarating, soon the speed became frightening.

Ahead he could hear Barney—first a whoop then a scream of excitement with a call of encouragement in between.

Then the slide disappeared beneath him, and Tim was propelled by his own momentum into an arch. He always wondered what it would be like to ski jump, and now he knew, although he wasn't all that thrilled by it. Now it was he who whooped and screamed. But he didn't fly much further. He landed in something soft and gooey, something that pulled him under.

Tim struggled. He tried to kick, but the goo held his legs immobile. He reached for whatever he could see in the dim light—rocks, trees, a limb or two hanging close. But he missed them all.

"Don't worry," Barney yelled as his voice gurgled beneath the goo.

"Don't worry? Are you nuts?" Tim shouted, but then he remembered—trust.

He relaxed and allowed himself to be sucked under. Although hard when it closed over his mouth and nose, it was harder still when he realized he was going to have to breathe. Lungs screaming, a natural fear of breathing underwater exploding within him, he finally took a deep breath. And took in air—great gulps of it.

Even though Tim's lungs were filled, he was still below the surface and the pressure was building as he headed toward the bottom—if there was a bottom.

That's when he felt his feet break through, kicking to free the rest of his body, he slowly dropped through the bottom of the ooze and joined Barney, who sat on the stone floor with his hands raised.

Hammond Helbert stood before them, a .357 Magnum leveled at them both.

Harve's little legs moved faster than Kelly thought they could. They crossed the floor of the cavern quickly to a cave on the other side. But rather than staying in the cave as they had done previously, when they came to a small waterfall, Harve dove through it. Kelly followed, and they came out in a very strange place.

Strings of lights hung everywhere while corridors branched in all directions. There were curious sounds—beeps, boops, a whir now and again.

"What's this?" Kelly asked.

"Pac Man," Harve called back. "You gotta keep moving in here."

"Pac Man?" Kelly cried. "That's old!"

"Helbert's a genius, but he's always been behind the times when it comes to games. He loves this one. We can get to this game from just about anywhere. Which means we can get to just about anywhere from it. It's a shortcut to the Thistle."

"What's the Thistle?"

"Where we're going."

"Why're we going there?"

But Harve didn't have time to answer, as a hockey puck with a voracious appetite came chomping toward them.

Kelly saw it, too, and started running—smack into a red fellow in a ghost outfit. He knocked her down. She got up just in time to turn and avoid the hockey puck, which went after the ghost.

Harve grabbed her hand. "This way," he said firmly.

There was another close call when the hockey puck and two more ghosts, a green and yellow one, nearly beheaded Harve as they ran over him. But Kelly and Harve soon worked their way across the game to a door marked: "Space Invaders."

Kelly gasped. "He plays Space Invaders?!"

"It relaxes him."

"But they shoot things."

"I told you this run isn't for the faint of heart."

"You never said that," Kelly protested, but Harve's hand went for the door handle.

"I didn't?" Harve questioned. "I meant to. Come on."

The door flew open.

Immediately squarish-looking projectiles aimed at saucer-shaped things beeped and booped past them. Harve leaped out of the way as one of them screamed by while Kelly ducked as one came so close it rustled her hair. They ran a few more steps, and one of the saucers dropped a bomb that skinned Kelly's arm. It hurt. "Hey," she said, "this isn't fun."

"I never found it much fun either. Now Donkey Kong . . ."

"We won't . . ."

"No, this is the last one." A bomb dropped inches from Harve while cannon fire caught him on the other side. Both missed, but Harve was obviously unnerved by the near misses.

Kelly had to jump out of the way as a saucer nearly landed on her. There was more cannon fire, more bombs. "We're at war," Kelly cried out to Harve, who ran with his hands cupped over his head.

"We sure are," Harve called back to her.

Another bomb! This one exploded near Harve and lifted him, short arms and legs flailing, against a cannon. He lay still for an instant.

Kelly turned back, more bombs dropping around her. "Are you hurt?" she cried.

"Just shaken," he shouted over exploding rounds.

Although Kelly had reached the exit door she scrambled back to help her little friend. She deftly dodged a couple of explosions and scooped an arm around Harve's back, helping him to his feet. Within seconds he ran alongside her again.

They flung open the exit door just as two bombs detonated in back of them. The force knocked them through the narrow opening and into a dense jungle. When the door latched shut the sound of explosions abruptly and completely died. They were left with jungle sounds of birds and monkeys and the guttural screech of a nearby cat.

"Through here?" Kelly groaned.

"He never finished this part."

"What's that mean?"

"I'm not sure," said Harve. "I guess we'll find out soon."

"Where you go, I go," Hammond hissed, the gun moving between Tim and Barney.

"Is this the intruder Dr. Helbert spoke of?" Barney asked, not terribly disturbed by the gun.

"He's the one," Tim said. He didn't like the gun at all.

"You spoke to Matthew?" Hammond seemed surprised.

"We did," Barney said with a note of triumph. Tim thought the little fellow's tone a bit premature.

That's when Tim noticed Barney's wand was missing.

"Well, no matter. Let's go," Hammond said.

"Where?" Tim asked.

"Since the squirt dropped through the ooze first, I would think he's leading. That right, squirt?" Hammond said.

"Barney's th' name. An' I am leadin'."

"Then lead on."

Tim hesitated, then said with an air of superiority, "Barney, I've noticed something that may be important here. When one of us who's visiting from the outside, like Mr. Helbert and me, comes in contact with another, we just pass through. I think the software creates the image, but not the substance behind it. So I don't think we're in any danger from . . . "

The .357 Magnum fired, and the bullet smashed into the wall next to Tim's head. The rock splintered and a fragment bit his ear—the same ear the Cruncher had hit, and it hurt.

"Part of my brother's system is an arsenal of weapons that

those who know about it, like me, for instance, can call on. The gun's a fake, a drawing. Which means in here it's very real."

Barney rubbed his brow. "Fascinatin' philosophical discussion, gents, but time's a wastin'. I 'ave me orders. On to the Thicket."

"Thicket? We have to go back there?" Hammond frowned, but then waved his gun. "Okay, let's get on with it."

Barney nodded and took the lead. Tim followed him and Hammond brought up the rear, the gun firmly in hand. They were in a cave. It looked much like the one Kelly and Harve had walked through earlier. It was dimly lit, with turns every several yards; now and then droplets of water plopped and it seemed to have no end.

Their pace wasn't as quick as it had been; Barney seemed to be taking his time. Soon Tim knew why. He could see Barney working the wand out the side of his trousers from the hip. He must have shoved it down there while descending the slide or squirming through the ooze.

Once he held it firmly he glanced back at Tim. Tim was ready. The moment they made their next turn, Barney rounded it first and when hidden from Hammond, spun, and waited for Tim to step by. Then he aimed at Hammond and shouted, "Hallelujah." Nothing happened.

Hammond raised his gun and fired, but not before they had dived behind a boulder.

"Aim at the rock near him," Tim ordered.

Barney did, and shouted "Hallelujah" again. This time the side of the cave near Hammond erupted and showered him with rock. Stunned, he reeled under the impact.

This gave Tim and Barney enough time to run, and run they did. The sand beneath their feet crunched, and they ricocheted off boulders as they rounded each turn. "Fire another one to try to block his path," Tim told Barney.

Barney did and the cave exploded in back of them, sending a dense avalanche of rock down from the ceiling. The cave was closed off.

They kept running, but slowed a bit to catch their breath. "How far now?" Tim asked.

"At the end," Barney gasped.

They rounded another turn and Hammond stood before them. "Drop the wand!" he ordered.

Tim didn't wait. He grabbed the wand and aimed nearly straight up. "Hallelujah," he shouted, and the roof of the cave burst and fell. He and Barney fell back just as a ton of rock collapsed.

"But there's no way out of here," Barney exclaimed. "It's closed up back there too."

"Think, Barney. Can you really get into a place in a computer program and not get out?"

"Sure," said Barney, "it's easy. We might be in a loop here. We might have to walk back and forth between these two piles of rubble forever."

Tim groaned. Maybe he'd outsmarted himself again.

□

The incessant clucks of monkeys and the caw of birds became almost more than Kelly could take, but the going was easy. There seemed to be only plants to brush aside and although the sounds indicated that animals were near, none showed themselves.

Until the ants.

Each big as a jungle cat, they walked along in single file across the path and carried huge things, like coconuts, bananas, and gourds.

That was strange enough, but then they heard an elephant trumpet. The nearby call accompanied the thunder of elephant feet, and the ground shook as they approached. Kelly and Harve looked for hiding places. But when the elephants arrived they were the same size as the ants, which were the same size as the big cats.

"Do you suppose that cat we heard back there is as big as an elephant?" said Kelly.

"Let's hope the size of an ant," Harve said. "Dr. Helbert must not have calculated the animals' size parameters yet."

"What else do you think he forgot?" Kelly asked.

Hammond stepped from behind a large tropical leaf, "He forgot to keep me out."

Kelly knew him immediately. Since Dr. Helbert's warning, she'd been expecting him.

"May I come along?" he asked with seeming politeness.

"No." Kelly tried to sound firm, but she had no idea how she could keep him from following if he wanted.

"I'll come anyway."

"You'll slow us down," Kelly said, "and you surely don't want to do that. You did say time was important."

"You heard from Helbert, too, didn't you?"

"Too? How did you . . . Tim. You know where Tim is."

"I do. Indeed I do. He'll be tied up for a bit."

Kelly didn't like the sound of that. "What do you mean?"

"Later," Hammond said. "Let's get going. We haven't much time."

"I'm sorry, sir," Harve spoke up, "but I'm under instructions to take no one to our destination except Kelly Craft. If you insist on coming, we don't go." Harve crossed his arms and looked as defiant as a dwarf could.

Hammond produced a very large handgun and pressed the barrel to Harve's head.

"Good to have you along, sir," Harve said with a weak smile. With his eyes darting toward the gun barrel, he began walking toward the ants.

"Whoa!" Hammond said, eyes wide with the large creatures. "Where you going?"

"We have to go that way."

"Oh," Hammond said and fired. One ant reeled under the force of the bullet's blow and dropped to the ground while the others scattered. "See, it's good I came along."

"I can see that right off," Harve said, taking the lead. Kelly walked between them.

Hammond eased up next to her and kept a strong eye on Harve. At one point he tried to take Kelly's hand, but his hand slipped through her image.

The jungle gave way to a field of rocks and boulders and a sheer cliff that rose to the sky next to them.

Suddenly Harve looked up, his face turned to panic—then

he pointed and screamed. Kelly instinctively ducked and Hammond did the same. Just as suddenly, Harve grabbed Kelly's hand and pulled her forward.

They heard the Magnum fire, but before Kelly knew anything else, Harve had dragged her inside the cliff—not into a cave, not behind anything, but right into the cliff. Thank goodness he kept hold of her hand because everything was black. Immediately ahead she heard Harve call back to her, "Keep running. It's all right. We're in stone."

"What?" Kelly asked, uncomfortable running this fast without being able to see.

"The last thing Dr. Helbert does is give the stones and things rigidity," Harve's voice explained. "That way he can go in and out without stopping until he finishes the program. He hasn't done that here yet. Now we can do the same."

Outside the cliff Hammond had an inkling what had happened. He pushed his hand into a nearby rock to make sure. There was no use following. He couldn't see them at all, and when he checked out their address on his display he saw that they were moving unusually fast. He decided to put the display on "Auto Check" and watch the address change. He could wait. When they stopped he'd nail them again.

CHAPTER 22

"Maybe we could blast the rock away," Tim suggested as he paced worriedly.

Barney rested against a boulder and picked his teeth with his pinky nail.

"That's gross," Tim groaned, desperate to unload on somebody. But then he heard a voice in the back of his head whisper, *God's in control.*

"Even in a tight loop," Tim reaffirmed and the thought gave him comfort.

"What?" Barney asked.

"I was saying that God's in control. Which means we're going to get out of here."

"Anythin' you say, Gov'n'ah," Barney said flatly as he continued picking.

Tim grabbed the wand.

"Whatcha gonna do wi' 'at?" Barney asked.

"Find some shelter," Tim commanded, and Barney moved quickly behind a rock. Tim slipped behind a boulder of his own and aimed at the pile of rubble that kept them from going forward and shouted, "Hallelujah."

The wand fired, the rocks exploded, dust and more rubble showered them, but no opening appeared.

"I could o' told ya. There's no place for all 'at t' go. Those are new rocks. They ain't gonna go back up."

Tim nodded thoughtfully. "They did fall down, didn't

they?" he stated as another thought occurred to him. "Barney, move back a bit," he instructed.

Barney seemed to have a healthy respect for Tim's unpredictability and did exactly as he was told. When he was safely away, Tim fired the wand again, this time just above the current pile. Another cave-in occurred, but this time they could see room above the rock pile.

Barney stood and registered surprised understanding. "I see what yer doin'," he said.

Before long, after some careful wand engineering, Tim had created a new cave above the rubble. As the rocks fell to the cave floor, an area opened up on top. He and Barney climbed up over the pile and, after kicking a bit of the rubble away from the end of their new cave, they were free again.

Now beyond the barrier, Tim heaved a great sigh of relief, "Time's going by. Lead the way, Barney."

After a quick glance of admiration, Barney began to run. Tim followed, and together, sometimes side by side, sometimes single file, they raced through the cave, a renewed sense of mission flooding their hearts.

Kelly shouted to Harve, "Where we going? Can you see in here?"

"We should break out of here any minute." Harve said, gasping for air.

Suddenly Kelly heard him hit something and just as suddenly she did too. It was a wall. They'd both plowed into it, and they both fell back—their hands no longer clasped together. They'd lost touch with one another!

"Harve, don't move," Kelly shouted. The panic she felt at the top of a crumbling rock bridge was nothing compared to the panic she felt now being lost in stone.

"I won't. We must have run into the back of something rigid."

"How do we get out?" Kelly questioned.

Harve thought a moment then said, "We walk along the wall until we find an opening."

"Sounds reasonable, but we need to find each other."

"Keep talking. I should be able to find you that way."

And he did. His arms swung in front of him, and he quickly came in contact with Kelly's leg. She immediately grabbed his arm, worked down to his hand, and said in relief, "You don't know how good you feel."

Tim and Barney ran as quickly as they could. The cave walls had long ago become a black blur. Each turn brought renewed hope that they'd see the tunnel's end. But so far each turn had disappointed them. They just kept running.

Hammond had been watching the address bits change. The zeros and ones down at the end spun quickly like a car's odometer. He finally saw them abruptly stop, then shuffle back and forth a bit, then move very slowly again. He watched, hand resting on the Magnum, and waited for what he thought would be just the right moment.

Kelly's left hand felt the smooth surface in front of them and her right held tightly to Harve's left. Harve was in the lead, his right hand feeling along the surface as they walked. "Where are we?" Kelly asked anxiously.

"I have my hopes."

"You mean you might be lost?"

"I've been lost before. There are parts of my personality, sort of a consistent pessimism, that Dr. Helbert worked long and hard with me to overcome. I would get lost because I'd be worrying too much about things."

"Are you worried about things now?" Kelly asked.

"I've been running in a rock, for crying out loud. Wouldn't you be a bit worried about that?"

"You have a point," Kelly admitted.

Suddenly Harve's hand pushed out and he felt something—nothing.

With a whoop of joy, the little man emerged from inside the rigidity to outside. Kelly quickly followed. Her eyes burned with the light, but it was a small price to pay for finally being outside of "inside" again.

Even though being outside was a great relief, it didn't look all that inviting. They had stepped through an opening in a cliff and now stood on a very narrow ledge. The ledge overlooked the deepest, most uninviting canyon Kelly had ever seen.

"Doesn't the good doctor know anything else but caves and canyons?" Kelly complained, then glanced down into a bottomless gorge. Immediately, she slammed herself against the cliff in back of her. If she hadn't, the vertigo would have pulled her down into the great abyss.

Unaware of her fear, Harve pointed at something growing out of the canyon and nearer the other side.

"What is that?" Kelly asked.

"The Thistle," Harve replied.

Out from the bottomless gorge, about halfway to the other side, grew a single, immense thistle, or what could have been called a thistle. Actually, it looked like a large pear-shaped object perched on the end of a thick green stem—the stem disappeared into the blackness of the gorge, as if the plant was rooted at the bottom of something bottomless. The pear-shaped thing on top was covered with spikes—spikes the size and shape of the thorns in the thicket. They were two to three feet long, very sharp, and about six inches apart.

Kelly's attention was suddenly pulled away. She heard two sets of running footsteps and the sounds of grunting and panting.

She plastered herself against the wall next to the opening from which she and Harve had emerged. The running slowed as it neared. Was it Hammond? She braced herself and was trying to figure out how she could defend herself when a wonderfully familiar face emerged from the cave. "Tim!" she cried and wrapped her arms around his neck.

Equally glad and equally surprised, Tim wrapped his long arms around her as well. Both Barney and Harve had to grab them before their exuberance took them over the edge.

"Oh, it's so great to see you," Tim said as seriously as he knew how. "I thought you'd flown away. Hammond told me he'd seen you."

"We'll have to talk all this over," Kelly said, becoming all business. "But right now I think we need to find out how to get in that thing."

Barney and Harve spent little time greeting one another and quickly turned their attention to the task at hand.

Tim eyed them both. "Okay, how?"

Barney smiled, "I'm not sure yer gonna lak 'is," he said.

Harve continued, "See these?"

For the first time Kelly and Tim saw two vines. The ends closest to them were draped over a rock, one on either side of the cave. What made the vines so extraordinary was that the opposite ends extended and disappeared into the sky, just above the thistle.

"Skyhooks," Tim laughed. He felt free to laugh for the first time in a long while. He never knew how much he cared for Kelly until he'd seen her again.

"Well, sort o'," Barney said. "But 'at's not important."

"You need to swing over to the Thistle," Harve said gravely.

"But the thorns," Kelly protested.

"What did Dr. Helbert say?" Harve asked.

Suddenly a gunshot echoed, and a bullet whined against a rock on the edge of a cave entrance. The rock shattered, and a piece of it nicked Kelly's shoulder. Her shirt tore and blood oozed from the scrape. She instantly gasped and grabbed her shoulder.

"All right, so it's in there." Hammond stood on an outcropping above them, his large gun pointed and ready to blast away again.

Kelly's shoulder stung, but not enough to stop her.

She eyed Tim, who eyed her back. Their minds one, each grabbed a vine, wrapped it around their wrists, and swung.

The gun thundered and bullets screamed as they burned past. Some came very close as Tim and Kelly leaped into the air. The vines held them, and as each saw the huge thorns coming toward them they reacted differently. Tim closed his eyes, and Kelly turned to the side. Neither reaction mattered.

All three who watched—Hammond, whose gun pumped bullet after bullet in their direction, Barney, who turned away and looked with a wince back at them over his shoulder, and Harve, who cupped his fingers over his eyes and peeked through his slightly spread fingers—gasped as the two kids were horribly impaled on the thorns.

"Ugh!" Barney groaned.

"My word!" Harve turned away.

Even Hammond couldn't believe what he'd seen. "That couldn't have happened. No, that couldn't have happened." Yet when he monitored them on his display, their addresses had stopped.

"Yuk!" he finally said. Then he argued, "No, that couldn't have happened."

It hadn't.

The kids swung at the thorns, and when they hit they kept on going. After a sensation of breaking through, they landed on a cushioned floor inside. The room was small and round and in the middle of it stood a single pedestal. But even though it was at the center of the room, the pedestal was not what caught their eye. The disembodied head of Dr. Matthew Helbert hung in the room before them. It spoke: "Please, push the button on the top of the pedestal."

"Touch that button and you're dead." Hammond suddenly stood behind them, the Magnum leveled in their direction. "I knew you'd made it in here. He shielded the room from monitoring. But I found it. Now to find the formula. It's got to be in here somewhere, and you're going to help."

The gun moved from side to side, first aimed between Kelly's eyes, then between Tim's.

But victory wasn't Hammond's this day. Suddenly Harve and Barney burst through the wall, feet extended, and caught Hammond in the small of his back. The gun fired wildly and flew from his hand. Tim pounced on it as he screamed to Kelly, "Hit the button. Quick!"

She took two rapid steps and all but fell on the red button. The moment she felt it depress beneath her hands, Matthew Helbert's face smiled. "Thank you," he said and disappeared. The instant the button was depressed, a digital coded message was sent to a nearby real fax machine.

Tim held the gun steadily on Hammond, "Now it's our turn . . . "

"No, I think not. You won," Hammond smiled coolly, ". . . this time." And he reached over and pressed his palm, then disappeared.

"He's gone!" Tim cried.

Kelly stepped over to him and hung a weary arm on his shoulders. "I hope pushing that button did some good."

"We'll find out soon, I guess."

The two of them eyed their companions. "I hate to be rude—you guys have been great, but we have things to find out about. We have to say good-bye," Tim said to Harve. "I don't think I caught your name in all the excitement."

"Harve," the little person said, reaching up a hand to shake Tim's.

"I'll miss you, Harve," Kelly smiled, shaking his hand.

"And I you," Harve smiled.

"How'd you guys get over here anyway?" Kelly finally asked.

"We saw 'im go," Barney said.

"And once you were in here, we could follow you," Harve explained.

Kelly nodded with all the understanding she needed.

"Ready?" Tim asked her.

"Ready," she replied, and together they pushed their palms.

◪

Dr. Ambrose Wittier of Scripps Research and Clinic, a frequent colleague of Dr. Matthew Helbert, got quickly on the phone to the FBI, as he'd been instructed to do by the fax he'd just received.

"Hello," Dr. Wittier said to the receptionist who'd answered, "is a . . . uh . . . Mike Dunhill there, please?"

Another voice got on the phone. "This is Agent Dunhill's chief. He's on assignment."

"I have something here that I think Mr. Dunhill wants. It came from Dr. Matthew Helbert and describes what appears to be a bacterium and what is labeled 'the cure.' He says in the fax that Agent Dunhill would want this."

There was a stunned silence on the other end of the line. Then he heard, "He does—yes, definitely. We'll be right over."

CHAPTER 23

Although Kelly found the instinctive part of her fear still in operation, the irrational part had waned a bit as she, Tim, and Uncle Morty flew into Minneapolis and then on to the Eau Claire airport.

The same two FBI agents who originally drove them to the airport met them. Although there were no warm hugs and kisses as there would have been had their parents been there, it still felt very good to be home again. It felt even better when they drove up to Uncle Morty's farm.

"I guess they weren't able to save the barn," Tim said, unloading his suitcase from the trunk. Indeed they hadn't. Where once Morty's proud blue barn had stood, now only blackened remains lay scattered about. Here and there a board or two still stood. Burned to within a few feet of the ground, they looked like charred gravestones.

As the car drove off, Kelly noticed a note tacked to the front door. Setting her suitcase down, she grabbed it. "It says the volunteer fire department feels really bad. When people found out which barn was burning they could only muster half their people."

"Everybody's a critic," Morty groaned. Getting out his keys he unlocked the door. But before he stepped inside a spark of life returned to his eyes, and he turned toward the black smudge where his barn used to be. "What if we build the next one in the form of a big cow? The hay loft could be the head and . . . "

"What about the Trojan Chicken?" Tim injected.

"I think you're getting the hang of this." Morty grinned. "Well, let's get inside and rest a bit. We'll worry about art in the morning."

Suddenly from around the back of the house came the howls of the dogs. Without stopping to say hello, the canines bolted around the side of the house in hot pursuit of Shivers, the big, caramel-colored cat.

Morty found another laugh. "I guess not much has changed after all."

Inside, Kelly went straight for the answering machine. The message indicator light was blinking quickly.

"You listen to the messages," Morty said. "I'm going to lie down. Comas really take the wind out of you."

"If there's anything interesting, I'll be upstairs unpacking," Tim told her as he headed up the steps.

A few minutes later Kelly came up. "One of the messages was from the church teen group," she said. "They're planning a party at the lake this Saturday night."

"I wonder if Cassy Briggs'll be there," Tim said, trying to make it sound like an idle question.

"I wouldn't be surprised," Kelly said. "A party at the lake sounds fun."

After a moment's hesitation, Tim said, "I guess we've learned some things, huh?"

"Some," Kelly nodded, sitting on the bed next to him. "It wasn't so much what I learned, but what I did. I faced my fears—I flew in a plane, walked over a crumbling bridge. What I did learn was Jesus is there with us—in that plane and on that bridge."

"And I guess I learned that I need to act a little more like God's son," Tim said, then added, "And that Cassy Briggs isn't all that bad."

Kelly laughed. Then she got to her feet. "I'll see you later. I have to unpack."

"Right. Later."

◻

A couple of hours passed, and Kelly felt restless. Unable to get through even the first page of a book she'd taken with her on the trip, she eased off her bed and went back to Tim's room. She found him in the exact same position she had left him in. He lay on his bed, his hands cupped behind his head, his eyes staring off into space.

"You okay?" Kelly asked.

"I couldn't believe it when Dr. Helbert said what we did."

Uncle Morty appeared at the door. "He said you saved humankind. And his own life."

Kelly felt a sudden surge of excitement. "And that bacterium can fight leukemia."

"That's why he didn't just destroy the microbe," Morty said, stepping into the room. "You guys okay?"

"How about you?" Kelly asked, "You looked like death warmed over all the way home."

"Felt like it too." Morty smiled.

"Can you believe we did all that?" Tim asked, eyes still very far away. "We saved thirty-two people—incredible! I want to tell everybody. "

"I wish the government would let us talk about it," Kelly said.

"Do you think anyone will ever thank us personally?" Tim asked, a certain disappointment in his voice.

The phone rang in the hallway. Kelly was halfway there before it rang twice. "Hello."

"May I speak to—uh—Kelly Craft?" It was a young voice, a little hesitant.

"This is me."

"My name is Tanya Walsh. Is your brother—Tim, isn't it?—there too? Is there any way I can talk to both of you?"

Kelly motioned for her brother to share the receiver.

He pressed his ear next to hers.

"Tim's here," Kelly said.

"You saved my mom," Tanya began, the tears evident in her voice. "She nearly died, but you guys came through just in time. She's all I've got, and now she's okay again. I had to thank you."

"Sure," said Tim. "Sure."

There were a few more words between them, but soon Kelly and Tim stood over a silent phone. "It doesn't feel like

I thought it would," Tim said. "God did it—through us—but he did it. I need to remember that."

Kelly nodded. "Me too."

"It's humbling for a Christian to do something extraordinary."

Kelly slapped the book she'd been reading into the palm of her hand. "You want to know what else is extraordinary? I don't know if I want to travel so much. It was fun, but real exotic places don't hold a candle to Helbertland."

"Maybe we'll be able to go back one day," Tim mused.

"We'd have to get a top secret clearance and tunnel into Fort Meade." Uncle Morty laughed softly.

"It might be worth it," Tim said, then he became serious. "Jesus was in there with us, wasn't he, Uncle Morty?"

Kelly answered, "He's always with us."

Morty's brows furled. "There's something else I'd like you guys to think about."

"What's that?" Tim asked.

"When you're unsaved, you're always living in virtual reality," Uncle Morty said. "What you see isn't all that's there. But more important, the reasons things seem to happen aren't always the real reasons. True reality has the Lord in it and until you're saved, you don't know that. Only after you climb out of the black suit and see things as they really are—see the Lord at work with his people and in his creation—do you see reality."

Tim nodded. "That might be a little deep for us farm kids. Right, Kelly?"

"Right. It's way too deep!" She laughed and continued, "What do you think our crazy uncle's going to get us mixed up in next?"

"What's this crazy uncle stuff?" Uncle Morty asked, taking mock offense.

"Maybe something to do with global warming," Tim tossed back.

"Or maybe fruit canning."

"Fruit canning. I think you're onto something!" Morty exclaimed.

"I understand canned fruit blows up sometimes," Tim volleyed.

"Only if you don't put the caps on right. Can you imagine a huge can of fruit with the lid on wrong? We'd be called to disarm it—now there's a job for a couple of farm kids," Kelly laughed and both kids jumped their uncle. They didn't stop laughing until he went to take a nap nearly an hour later.

After Uncle Morty had left, Tim followed Kelly into her room. "Well, sis . . ." he started. They'd been through a lot together in the past few days. They'd grown up a little and grown a lot closer. He wasn't sure how to tell her that she meant a lot to him and the past few days had shown him just how much. Instead he shuffled self-consciously and said, "I'll see you in the morning."

"A bunch of us are getting together later—about eight—to plan the party. Bonnie called."

"Cassy going to be there?"

"I think so."

"See you at eight," Tim said and went down the hall.

Kelly heard his door close and picked up her book without looking at it. Crickets rattled outside, a squadron of fireflies dipped and bobbed by her bedroom window, and a cool breeze slipped in. It felt a little like rain. The farm wasn't all that bad, she thought—peaceful, steady.

Tim slipped into bed and grabbed a puzzle book. He worked for a second or two on a logic problem, but then set it down, pondering a greater one. How could he get into Fort Meade and back into VR? He couldn't do it through Hammond's remote suit; that connection had been disconnected. He'd have to do it legally—no lies—as a Christian. How could he do it?

Suddenly the phone rang. Leaping to his feet he collided with Kelly in the hallway. She got to it first and pushed the receiver to her ear. "Mom? . . . Sure, we're all right. . . . You'll never guess what happened. . . . No, Uncle Morty's cow's fine. . . . We went to virtual reality . . . Disneyland? Sure, Mom, it's sort of like Disneyland . . . "

ABOUT THE AUTHOR

Bill Kritlow was born in Gary, Indiana, and moved to northern California when he was nine. He now resides in southern California with his wife, Patricia. They have three daughters and five grandchildren. Bill is also a deacon at his church.

After spending twenty years in large-scale computing, Bill recently changed occupations so that he could spend most of the day writing—his first love. His hobbies include writing, golf, writing, traveling, and taking long walks to think about writing. In addition to *A Race Against Time,* Bill has also written *Driving Lessons* and *Crimson Snow*.

An excerpt from *The Deadly Maze,* Book Two in the Virtual Reality Series:

Tim and Kelly, on a frantic quest to find the means to release the President of the United States and Uncle Morty from virtual reality before Hammond Helbert destroys them, find themselves on a virtual space station with a real problem.

"What happens when a meteor hits a space station?" Kelly asked, eyeing the meteor from the bridge's panoramic viewscreen as it grew closer.

The voice came back. "Impact in three minutes—impact point: the bridge."

Four shocked eyes locked together.

"We've got to get out of here."

Charging the door, they threw it open and dove down the vertical tube they found there. They grabbed at its walls and walked their hands down it. Their progress was slow; three minutes must have ticked away already, but they obviously had not. Tim and Kelly clawed at the wall again and again until they reached the axle door. It was locked.

The voice sounded another warning: "Thirty seconds to impact. We've got a real problem here, trainees."

Frantic, Kelly joined her brother who was working on the door. Moving beside him, she pushed against the panel just above the door. It gave way!

Kelly instinctively dove through it. Tim followed, and Kelly slammed the panel shut. She heard it latch.

Where were they? They didn't know for sure, but they knew this section of the station was committed to agriculture. Crops were planted as far as they could see—some were familiar, some were not—corn, soy beans, wheat, even trees and flowers. Arcing above them was a glass roof through which they saw the meteor strike.

The meteor itself was just a streak, a blurred bullet blazing through space. Then it hit the station.

First, it slammed into one of the cross tubes connecting the wheels. In a heartbeat, the tube exploded. Steel girders ripped and twisted like spaghetti; panels that defined the tubes' walls shattered and were thrown off into space; tongues of flame erupted but quickly died from lack of oxygen, blackening the tubes' ragged edges. A few of the exploding panels spun like power saw blades cutting into an adjacent tube. The pressure inside the tube blew out the panels near the cut and then exploded as electricity, chemicals, and gases merged. More flames, more charring.

The meteor continued on through another connector tube. Great portions immediately disintegrated. Molten metal spewed out, following the meteor, then larger pieces broke loose—jagged edges, swirling and twisting against the black. Finally, whole panels tore free—white squares also twisted and flew off. Debris followed the meteor as it plunged toward earth, having wreaked all the havoc it could on *Freedom IV.*

"What now?" Kelly gasped.

Tim shook his head, still awestruck by the destructive power he had just witnessed. "Whatever it is, we'd better do it quickly. The space station is breaking up."